"Get out o

Like lightning to a rod, ~~his blue eyes~~ on her bare shoulders and silky white negligee.

Scowling, Lindsey pulled up the covers around her neck. "Go away, Alex. I think we've both said enough for one evening—"

"You're right," he said, surprising her by agreeing. "We've said too much. That's the problem."

With his shirt unbuttoned and his shirt cuffs rolled up to reveal strong forearms, he looked disheveled and dangerous.

Lindsey shivered with trepidation.

He stepped closer to her bed. "I said some things that were totally out of line. I don't know what came over me."

She knew. They were in a romantic paradise, alone for the first time in their lives without a chaperone.

"Still friends?"

She nodded. He sighed his relief. "Thank goodness."

Then, before she knew what was happening, he enveloped her in a hug…. Liquid heat spilled through her veins. Alex was putting her through hormonal hell.

He pulled away, but didn't release her. For a moment she was afraid he might kiss her.

Afraid he wouldn't.

Dear Reader,

In 20 months Silhouette Romance will celebrate its 20th anniversary! To commemorate that momentous occasion, we'd like to ask *you* to share with us why you've chosen to read the Romance series, and which authors you particularly enjoy. We hope to publish some of your thoughtful comments during our anniversary year—2000! And *this* month's selections will give you food for thought.…

In *The Guardian's Bride* by Laurie Paige, our VIRGIN BRIDES title, a 20-year-old heiress sets out to marry her older, wealthy—gorgeous—guardian. Problem is, he thinks she's too young.… *The Cowboy, the Baby and the Bride-to-Be* is Cara Colter's newest book, where a shy beauty reunites a lonely cowboy with his baby nephew…and lassoes love in the process! Karen Rose Smith's new miniseries, DO YOU TAKE THIS STRANGER?, premieres with *Wealth, Power and a Proper Wife*. An all-work-and-no-play millionaire learns the value of his marriage vows when the wife he'd suspected of betraying him suffers a bout of amnesia.

Rounding out the month, we have *Her Best Man* by Christine Scott, part of the MEN! promotion, featuring a powerful tycoon who heroically offers protection to a struggling single mom. In *Honey of a Husband* by Laura Anthony, an ex-bull rider returns home to discover his childhood sweetheart is raising *his* child—by another woman. Finally, rising star Elizabeth Harbison returns to the lineup with *True Love Ranch*, where a city gal and a single-dad rancher lock horns—and live up to the Colorado spread's name.

Enjoy!

Joan Marlow Golan

Joan Marlow Golan
Senior Editor Silhouette Romance

Please address questions and book requests to:
Silhouette Reader Service
U.S.: 3010 Walden Ave., P.O. Box 1325, Buffalo, NY 14269
Canadian: P.O. Box 609, Fort Erie, Ont. L2A 5X3

HER
BEST MAN

Christine
Scott

Silhouette
R O M A N C E™
Published by Silhouette Books
America's Publisher of Contemporary Romance

To Mom—
a truly gentle woman

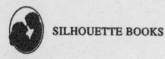 SILHOUETTE BOOKS

ISBN 0-373-19321-1

HER BEST MAN

Copyright © 1998 by Susan Runde

This edition published by arrangement with Harlequin Books S.A.

Books by Christine Scott

Silhouette Romance

Hazardous Husband #1077
Imitation Bride #1099
Cinderella Bride #1134
I Do? I Don't? #1176
Groom on the Loose #1203
Her Best Man #1321

CHRISTINE SCOTT

grew up in Illinois but currently lives in St. Louis, Missouri. A former teacher, she now writes full time. When she isn't writing romances, she spends her time caring for her husband and three children. In between car pools, baseball games and dance lessons, Christine always finds time to pick up a good book and read about…love. She loves to hear from readers. Write to her at P.O. Box 283, Grover, MO 63040-0283.

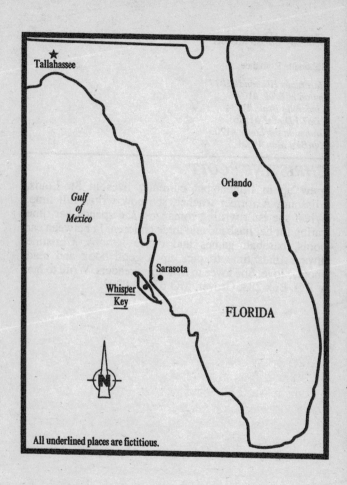

Tallahassee

Orlando

Gulf
of
Mexico

Sarasota

Whisper
Key

FLORIDA

N

All underlined places are fictitious.

Prologue

"Bartender, another drink for me and my friends," Alex Trent called.

Happy hour had long gone. The dinner rush was finally winding down for the evening. All that was left in the bar were a few stragglers, stopping off for an after-dinner drink and quiet conversation. Alex and his group of friends were the boisterous exception to the rule.

But, hell, Alex mused, why not?

Tonight was a celebration, wasn't it?

His best friend was getting married to the only woman Alex would ever love. He couldn't think of a better reason to get stinking drunk.

The bartender ambled toward Alex, assessing him as he went. "A Scotch, two drafts and a coffee, right?"

"That's right," he said with an emphatic nod. The words came out slow, and only slightly slurred.

"Looks like you guys are celebrating," the bartender observed. "What's the occasion?"

Determined not to let his bitterness show, he slapped

his closest drinking buddy on the back. "This is Danny boy's last weekend as a bachelor. The fool's about to take the plunge into matrimonial bliss."

"Danny boy"—sandy-haired, well over six feet and weighing close to one-eighty-five—grimaced. "Jeez, Alex, do you have to make an announcement everywhere we go?"

Alex ignored his friend. "Bartender, have you ever been married?"

"No, sir. I can't say that I have," he answered, placing a glass of Scotch on the bar top.

"Smart man," Alex said, helping himself to a hefty swig of the drink.

"Give it a rest, Alex," Danny muttered. "I'm not changing my mind."

"He'd better not," the largest of the group said, a seriously fit-looking man with thick, black hair and dark brooding eyes. "Otherwise he'll have to answer to me for breaking my little sister's heart."

A worried expression crossed Danny's face. "You've got nothing to worry about, Rick. No one, not even Alex and his big mouth, is going to talk me out of marrying Lindsey."

"Don't let Alex bother you, Danny," Jon, Alex's brother, advised with a chuckle. Jon was a taller, darker version of Alex. The family resemblance was uncanny. "He's still kicking himself for letting you get to Lindsey first."

Danny narrowed a glance at Alex. "That true?"

Alex felt his heart leap into his throat. Jon's observation hit too close to the truth. Scowling, he said, "You know, you've got a big mouth, brother." He returned his gaze to his friends, deftly changing the subject. "It's bad enough I have to see him everyday at work. Tell me again, why did we bring him along, tonight?''

"Because he was the only one crazy enough to agree to drive us anywhere we want," Rick explained.

The bartender shook his head.

"To designated drivers." Toasting his reprieve, Alex drained his Scotch. The liquid burned his throat. His eyes watered. But the drink had served its purpose. He felt blessedly numb inside.

Danny knocked elbows with Jon. "You're married, right, Jon? Tell 'em, marriage isn't so bad."

"Marriage isn't so bad," Jon repeated.

Alex snorted. "Spoken like a true believer."

"Come on, Jon," Danny pleaded. "Help me out here. Tell 'em the advantages of being married."

Jon sipped his coffee, looking as though he were giving the matter considerable thought. Then said, "Well, the food isn't bad. Much better than I could make myself."

Alex and Rick exchanged glances. Grinning, they chorused, "Takeout."

Jon took up the challenge. "Okay, how about companionship? Since I've been married, I've never had to come home to an empty house."

"Hell, Jon," Rick drawled. "If I want companionship, I can always get myself a dog."

Alex chuckled.

Jon continued, unperturbed. "Then there's the sex…when you're married, boys, you don't have to go looking for love."

Alex studied his drink, fighting an unwanted surge of jealousy.

Danny's tone brightened appreciably. "That's right. After this weekend, Lindsey and I—"

"Don't even think of mentioning my sister and sex in the same sentence," Rick warned him, a forbidding look on his face.

"Rick, your sister's a big girl now. She's getting married next week," Jon said, biting back an amused smile. "I think she knows all about the birds and the bees."

Rick pointed an unsteady finger at Alex's brother. "If it was your little sister we were discussing, you'd feel the same way."

"He's right, Jon," Alex murmured. "I don't know about you, but I haven't had a decent night's sleep since Stephanie started dating."

Rick frowned. "The brat's old enough to date?"

Alex and Jon shot their friend a disbelieving look. Alex was the first to speak. "The brat's in college. She's going to law school next fall."

"Law school? Why doesn't that surprise me?" Rick grunted, then proceeded to answer his own question. "She certainly has the mouth to be a lawyer. I've never met anyone as opinionated as your little sister." He shot Alex a wary glance. "No offense, Alex, but you know I've never been able to warm up to the brat."

"Don't worry, Rick," Alex assured him. "I believe the feeling's mutual."

Rick leaned back in his seat and grinned. "Like I always said, the only good thing to come of your parents moving to Florida was that they took your little sister along with them."

Alex gave a noncommittal shrug.

A thoughtful pause descended upon the group. They sipped their drinks in silence. The bartender wiped a rag over the bar, buffing the already-shiny surface.

After considerable deliberation, Alex announced,

"Boys, this party's getting entirely too quiet. I think it's time we moved on."

"Now where?" Jon groaned.

Alex stood. "The east side of the river. Where the entertainment's a little friskier...if you catch my meaning."

"Uh-uh." Danny shook his head. "I promised Lindsey I wouldn't go to any strip joints."

"After next weekend, you can do anything Lindsey tells you," Alex said, pulling Danny to his feet. "Tonight, you're with us."

The pair swayed slightly, looking none too steady.

Danny moaned, "Lindsey's gonna kill me if I get into trouble."

"Trouble? We're not going to get into trouble," Alex assured him. He patted Rick on the shoulder. "Not as long as we have a cop in the group."

"Alex, are you trying to influence a police officer?" Rick asked, striving for solemnity, but the words came out thick and slurred.

"Would I have any luck if I did?"

"Hell, no."

"Then there's your answer."

Rick chuckled.

"Alex, I don't think this is such a good idea," Danny said as he was led away, Rick on one side of him, Alex on the other.

"We're friends, Danny. Have I ever let you down?" Alex asked, trying not to dwell on the irony of his own words. Their friendship was the only reason he hadn't tried to stop this wedding. If it had been anyone else but Danny who'd proposed to Lindsey, he wouldn't have given a second thought to stealing her away. "Trust me,

Lindsey won't be upset. If she is, I'll take care of it. You can count on me, buddy."

"Mr. Responsibility, that's you, Alex..." Danny mumbled, his words fading as they stepped away.

Mr. Responsibility. The title struck a discordant note in Alex's fuzzy mind. Since freshman year in high school, they'd been the best of friends, each assuming their appointed roles. Rick, the athlete. Danny, the maniac. And Alex, Mr. Responsibility.

Alex had always been the one to clean up one or another of the messes Danny had gotten them into. Danny's reckless spirit had been impossible to tame. Which was why Alex had been stunned when his best friend had announced he was going to marry Lindsey.

Not that he didn't understand his friend's reason. Beautiful, gentle Lindsey held the power to reform even the worst of life's reprobates.

Regret rifled through him. If only...

Alex slammed the brakes on the thought, not allowing it to go another step. Lindsey, and whatever feelings he may have had for her, was in the past. He'd waited too long to tell her the truth...that he cared.

Now it was too late.

Dammit, it was much too late.

Chapter One

Four years later

The woman of his dreams was tall, slender and dark haired. Her back was turned to him as she stared out onto the ocean, giving him a mouthwatering view of shapely curves outlined in a sexy red dress. A light breeze softened the air, molding the silky material to her body.

Alex firmly believed he'd died and had gone to heaven. If not heaven, then surely he was in paradise.

Impatiently, he reached out, anxious to learn the identity of his dream woman. His fingers grazed the smooth skin of her shoulder, sending shock waves of awareness tripping through his body. And—

A bell rang.

The woman's image faded.

Alex moaned, fighting to hold on to the remnants of sleep. He hit the Snooze button on his clock radio. Once again, quiet descended upon his bedroom. With a sigh, he snuggled under the covers for another ten minutes of ecstasy.

The dark-haired enchantress resurfaced in his mind's eye and…the bell rang, again.

Not the radio, he realized. The phone was ringing.

Grumpily, Alex pried open his eyes and squinted at the clock radio. It was 6:00 a.m. *Who in their ever-loving mind would be calling him at this hour?*

Another ring.

Alex growled and yanked the receiver from its cradle, effectively stopping the shrill peal. "Speak to me," he mumbled as he closed his eyes and drifted back into oblivion.

"Alex?"

The woman of his dreams now had a voice. A vaguely familiar, sweet and sexy voice. The rich, velvety timbre reminded him of melt-in-your-mouth chocolate fudge. Alex licked his lips at the thought.

"Alex?" A trace of impatience this time. "Are you there?"

The woman of his dreams had a face. A perfect oval-shaped face with patrician features. Her eyes were the color of smooth, rich caramels, with only a touch of sadness tinging the mix. Her nose was pert and slightly upraised, as though she were ready to challenge his integrity. Smart girl. Her mouth…her mouth was like a strawberry, plump and ripe and ready for the picking.

His empty stomach growled a hungry protest.

"Alex, wake up!"

Startled, Alex sat up straight, knocking the bedcovers aside. Cold air hit his passion-aroused bare skin. He shivered in response. Just a dream, he told himself, shaking off the remnants of sleep. A dream that had been occurring much too often. What had been denied him in waking moments, his subconscious seemed bent on allowing him in slumber.

The woman of his dreams was Lindsey Richards, his best friend's wife.

"Lindsey?" he croaked, wincing at the strained sound of his voice.

"I was just about ready to give up on you, Alex," she said with an impatient breath.

Guilt lodged in his throat as he recalled his wanton dream and the major role his friend's wife had almost played in it. He swallowed hard. "Don't do that, Lindsey. You know I'm always here for you. Anytime you need me."

"I know that, Alex." Her tone softened. "You've been—" She paused, her voice catching. "You've been very good to me. More than I deserve—"

"Don't start that again." He scowled. They'd had this discussion before. It had happened with an annoying frequency in the past two years since Danny Richards had been tragically killed in a traffic accident. "I've told you before, we're friends." Though, if repressed desires had anything to do with it... He allowed the thought to go unfinished. "Friends look out for each other."

"I know that, Alex, but—" She gasped. "Goodness, what am I thinking? I forgot to ask. Is this a good time to talk? Or am I, uh, interrupting something?"

He feigned ignorance. "You mean, other than my getting a full night's sleep?"

"No, Alex, that's not what I mean." The impatience was back again. Alex could almost imagine her raising that pert little nose of hers. "I meant...are you alone?"

A blush probably accompanied that last hushed question. Alex couldn't help but smile. For a woman who'd been married and had given birth to a child, she was such an innocent.

"Hold on. Let me check." Alex took the opportunity to pull the wayward covers back up to his waist. Then, stacking his hands beneath his head and cradling the phone against his shoulder, he settled back onto the bed. "Nope, no one under these covers but little ol' lonesome me."

"Good," she said, sounding relieved. Alex raised a curious brow, wondering if she were relieved that they were free to talk or that she'd found him alone in his bed. Before he could ask, she continued, "I wanted to catch you before you went to work. Do you remember what day it is today?"

"Jeez, Lindsey. Do you have to give me a pop quiz at six o'clock in the morning?"

"Alex—"

"All right, all right...let's see, well, it's Friday. The third week in November. Thanksgiving's less than a week away. And—wait, I know there's something else— ah, yes, it's my godson's birthday."

"You remembered," she said, unable to keep the pleasure from her voice.

"How could I forget?" He chuckled. "Jamie's been reminding me of the upcoming event every time I've seen him in the last two months."

James Daniel Richards was the spitting image of his father. A towheaded hellion with an angel's smile. He had everyone who loved him wrapped around his chubby little finger. Alex included.

"Which brings me to the reason I called," she said, her discomfort obvious.

Warning signals prickled his skin. He waited.

"Alex, I don't want you to feel obligated to come tonight."

He sat up in bed again, nearly dropping the phone in his haste. "Lindsey—"

She wouldn't let him finish. "Hear me out, Alex. Jamie's been a little overly enthusiastic about his birthday. Turning three's an important step. When you're three, you're officially old enough to go to preschool. And chances are good that you're going to make a real haul with all those birthday presents." She stopped rambling long enough to suck in a deep breath. He could almost see the tiny furrow forming between her dark brows, the one she always got whenever she was feeling pensive. "The thing is, Alex, I'm sure you have better things to do with your time than spend a Friday night at a three-year-old's birthday party."

"Such as?" he demanded, his grip tightening around the receiver.

"Well...a date, for instance."

"You think I'd rather go on a date than attend my only godson's birthday party," he said, his voice low and deceptively even. Anger simmered beneath the surface of his calm demeanor. "Just what kind of godfather do you think I am?"

"You're a wonderful godfather," she assured him. "Too wonderful. That's the problem. What with work and your *busy* social life—"

"Busy social life?" Was that a note of jealousy he'd detected in her tone? Nah, he assured himself, just wishful thinking on his part. "What busy social life?"

"Oh, Alex, really," she said, laughing.

He felt his defenses kicking in. "All right, maybe I go out on a few dates—"

"A few? Tell me, Alex, is there any woman over the age of eighteen in St. Louis that you haven't dated?"

Though her tone was teasing, the question caught him off guard. So he went out on a few dates—okay, a lot of dates. Who could blame a man for trying to drown his sorrows in female companionship? Especially since the only woman he'd ever really wanted thought of him as nothing more than a *good friend.*

"Now, look, Lindsey—"

"I know, I know, your personal life is your own business." Lindsey sighed. "I never meant to criticize you. All I wanted to say was that, with everything else you have going on, I don't know how you find so much time to spend with Jamie. It's too much."

"I can handle it," he growled, finding his voice.

"Alex, Danny wouldn't expect you—"

"It's settled, Lindsey," he said in a tone that would brook no further argument. "I'm not skipping out on my godson's birthday party. Now what time should I be there?"

She hesitated. Then, in a resigned tone, said, "Seven o'clock. I'm afraid to make it any later. Or the guest of honor will be nodding off before he gets to open his presents."

"Seven o'clock will be fine," he said firmly.

"Alex, are you sure—"

"Lindsey, give me a break. It's too early for an argument. I haven't even had a cup of coffee yet."

He heard her soft sigh, a whispery breath across the phone line. "All right, Alex. I'll see you tonight."

"G'bye, Lindsey."

He waited, listening for the click of her phone to disconnect before he hung up the receiver. Once she was gone, the bedroom felt too quiet, too empty. He laid back on his bed and brooded over his conversation with Lindsey.

"Stubborn, fool woman," he muttered to the four walls. "She has enough to worry about. She doesn't need to add my social life to the list."

As usual, when it came to dealing with Lindsey, his anger quickly dissipated. These past two years hadn't been easy for her, he reminded himself. Danny's death had been unexpected. His loss was a devastating blow for all of them. For Lindsey, most especially.

She wasn't prepared, financially or emotionally, for the unspeakable. Typical of Danny, he'd believed himself to be invincible. He hadn't bothered with life insurance and he'd just socked away most of their savings in a down payment on a house, a rambling, old fixer-upper in Kirkwood. The house had great potential, a big yard, lots of room, a perfect home for a growing family. But it was also a money pit. Something always needed to be repaired. After Danny's death, Lindsey had been left scrambling to make ends meet.

Not that she would have admitted any of this to him.

The only way he'd found out about her monetary problems was through her brother, Rick. Alex's offer of financial assistance had been graciously yet firmly turned down. Instead, Lindsey chose to work two jobs on top of raising her son, just so she wouldn't lose the house that she held in loving tribute to her late husband.

The thought left a bitter taste in his mouth, one that he refused to attribute to jealousy. Long ago, Alex had accepted that any romantic feeling he may have toward Lindsey was merely an exercise in futility. Lindsey had loved Danny. She still loved him very deeply. Their being apart was a tragedy. Besides, how could he be jeal-

ous of his best friend, a man who'd been cheated out of
the best years of his life?

Alex shifted uncomfortably in his bed. Lindsey might
be too stubborn to accept a simple loan of money—a
loan that he could well afford to make—but he'd be
damned if his moral support would be brushed aside
with as much ease. As long as Lindsey and his godson
needed him, he intended to be there for them.

It was the least he could do for the widow of his best
friend.

The phone rang again.

Alex glared at the instrument. Lindsey, again. She'd
probably thought of a new excuse why he shouldn't
bother attending his own godson's birthday party. He
snatched the phone from its cradle.

"You know, it's a good thing I don't have a woman
in bed with me this morning," he growled. "I'd have a
hell of a time explaining all these phone calls if I did."

Dead silence met his terse greeting.

Then, after a discreet clearing of a feminine throat, an
older woman's voice responded, "Well, Alex, thank you
for sharing that bit of information with me. I'm not sure
whether I should be relieved or disappointed."

"Mom?" Alex moaned as he thunked a hand against
his forehead.

"Obviously, you were expecting someone else."

"Yes, I mean...no. Mom, do you have any idea what
time it is?"

"Yes, dear. It's ten minutes after seven in the morning."

"Seven o'clock Florida time, Mom. It's only six
here."

"I know that, dear. I didn't want to miss you before

you left for work." Her dismissive tone grated against Alex's nerves.

"I wanted to talk to you about next weekend. Remember? The wedding? You are coming, aren't you?"

"Of course, I'm coming. My baby sister's getting married. Did you think I'd miss it?"

"Well, I know how busy you and Jon have been lately." She clucked her tongue disapprovingly. "I still don't understand why you and Jon needed M.B.A.s to sell tennis shoes. But your father assures me you're both doing fine, and I shouldn't worry."

They were doing more than fine. Lobo Shoes, the company he and Jon had founded shortly after graduating from college, was the fastest growing athletic shoe company on the market. It wouldn't be long before they'd be giving Reebok and Nike a run for their money, no pun intended.

"Look, Mom—"

She never gave him a chance to finish. "I've been trying to get hold of Jon, but no one's answering at his house."

Alex sighed. "Jon's out of town. We're expanding into the West Coast market. He's making sure things go smoothly. I'm sure Jon said he'd be flying in with Rachel on Thursday for the wedding."

"And how about you, Alex? Will you be bringing anyone to the wedding? Anyone special?"

He grimaced at her hopeful tone. "No, Mom."

"Alex," she said, her disappointment obvious. "Your brother's been married almost five years. Now, even your younger sister is getting married. Don't you think it's time you stopped this galavanting around and found yourself a nice girl to settle down with?"

Alex groaned. First Lindsey. Now his mother. Why

was everyone suddenly so concerned about his social life?

At six o'clock in the morning, however, Alex wasn't up to an argument with his mother. "Yeah, Mom, maybe someday," he sighed. "Just as soon as I meet the right woman—"

"Alexander Hale Trent, you've been avoiding the marriage altar for so long, you wouldn't recognize the right woman if she were standing under your own nose."

Alex gritted his teeth.

She continued. "Now, there'll be plenty of eligible young women at the wedding. Do you remember Rosemary Plinkton? Stephanie's maid of honor? Her friend from college? She isn't married and she's such a sweet young thing. I'm sure you two will hit it off just fine—"

"Mom, don't even consider trying any matchmaking during the wedding." He assumed his most threatening tone. "Or I swear, it'll be the last time you'll see me in Florida."

"Oh, pooh," she said, not in the least bit intimidated. "Did anyone ever tell you you're awfully grumpy in the morning?"

Alex stifled a groan. "Mom, I've got to get ready for work."

"Of course, Alex," his mother trilled. "I'll see you on Wednesday. Have a wonderful day!"

The phone line clicked. Slowly, Alex returned the receiver to its cradle, staring at the instrument in disbelief. Had it really been only ten minutes ago when he'd been sound asleep in his bed, not a care in the world, enjoying what promised to be the most erotic dream of his life? It seemed like a lifetime ago.

Since awakening, he'd gotten into a disagreement with one of his best friends. And his mother had called to make her intentions clear. She was determined to see to it that the last of her unmarried children bit the matrimonial bullet.

Alex growled as he tossed the covers aside and pushed himself out of bed. A hell of a way to start out the morning. How could the day get any worse?

How could the day get any worse?

Lindsey Richards stared at the mess in her workroom and felt an overwhelming urge to cry. Spools of thread had been pulled from their racks. Yards and yards of the bright-colored strands were strewn about in jumbled heaps on the floor. Beads and bangles, all essential parts of her tassel-making craft business, glittered on the carpet like tiny jewels.

In the middle of this chaos sat the birthday boy himself, her three-year-old son, Jamie.

"James Daniel Richards," she began, struggling to control her temper. "What do you think you're doing in here?"

He looked up at her with his big blue eyes and said, "Playing."

"Where's your uncle Rick? He's supposed to be keeping an eye on you."

Jamie pointed a chubby finger toward the family room, where the sound of a football game playing on the TV filtered down the hall. Rick, her usually reliable brother. Lindsey sighed. These past few weeks the change in him seemed so daunting. He'd become moody and withdrawn, unwilling or unable to talk about the unfortunate incident that very well may have cost him his job. She was at her wit's end. She just didn't know how to help him.

"You know you aren't supposed to be in here," she reminded her son sternly.

"I'm sorry." Jamie's lower lip trembled slightly as he spoke. His eyes filled with unshed tears.

Lindsey's anger dissolved at the sight. How could she be angry with Jamie today of all days? It was his birthday, after all. She reached out a hand. "Come here."

Slowly, he untangled himself from a pool of thread and sauntered over to her, scuffing the toes of his tennis shoes on the carpet as he did so. At that moment, he reminded her so much of his father, he nearly took her breath away. Danny, too, had had trouble admitting when he was wrong.

Lindsey brushed the memory from her mind as Jamie took hold of her hand. He wouldn't quite meet her eyes. She knelt to be at eye level with her young hell-raiser. "Jamie, this is the room where Mommy works. I don't want you playing in here again, all right?"

He nodded, still unable to meet her gaze.

Glancing at the messy workroom, she sighed. "Give me a hug, honey. I sure could use one about now."

His face brightening, he wrapped his arms around her neck and squeezed with all his might. Despite feeling bone-tired, she couldn't help but smile. On a day like today, she needed the comfort of a warm, loving body.

"Hey, how about me?" A familiar, deep voice startled them. "Don't I get a hug, too?"

Alex stood in the hall, not two feet away, watching them with an amused expression on his face.

"Uncle Alex!" His mother forgotten, Jamie threw himself at the new arrival.

Pleasure and guilt warred as she watched Alex scoop the boy into his arms and endure one of Jamie's bone-cracking hugs. Pleasure because, with Alex and Rick

nearby, Jamie never lacked a positive male influence.
Guilt because, no matter how much she appreciated it,
she had no right to expect Alex's help.

"Where's my present?" Jamie demanded.

Alex chuckled. "In the dining room, with all the
rest."

Jamie wiggled himself out of Alex's arms. With the
speed of a heat-seeking missile, he catapulted himself
down the hall, beating a hasty path for the goodies.

Lindsey stood, shaking her head. "He really isn't as
materialistic as he seems."

"Of course he is," Alex said, still grinning. "He's a
kid, remember?"

Her heart thumped an uncertain beat as their gazes
connected across the width of hall. Alex seemed to fill
the narrow space with his presence. Tall and lean, blond-
haired and blue-eyed, his skin bronzed by hours out in
the sun, he was a walking spokesman for the benefits of
using his own athletic shoes. A diehard jogger, he looked
wonderfully fit and healthy, exuding a confidence and
an energy she didn't share.

"I didn't hear you arrive," Lindsey murmured, glancing away.

"Rick let me in."

"My brother's able to answer a doorbell," she muttered as she surveyed the damage caused by one small
boy. "But he can't keep an eye on his own nephew."

Alex stepped up behind her, glancing over her shoulder at the mess. He released a long whistle. His breath
tickled the sensitive skin at the back of her neck. "Did
Jamie do this?"

"Yep." With a sigh, she added, "Rick was supposed
to be watching him."

Alex hesitated. Then, with a nod toward the family

room where the TV still blared, he asked, "How is Rick?"

"Crabby, sulky…impossible. I swear, if he weren't my own brother, I'd refuse to see him until he was in a better mood." She felt an instant guilt at her lack of support and understanding. "The whole thing's crazy. I can't believe Rick might lose his job just because he issued a silly little traffic ticket."

Alex bit back a smile. "Well, I think there's more to it than that, Lindsey. There was the letter he wrote to the editor, the one questioning the department's policy of ticket fixing—"

Lindsey jumped to her brother's defense. "My father was a policeman, Alex. A darned good one, too. He taught us if you break the law, you pay the price. It's as simple as that. I don't care whose relative has taken offense to being stopped."

"Yeah, but the mayor's brother—"

"Look, Rick's *my* brother. And this is his life's work that's on the line. He looks haggard, Alex. I don't think he's getting much sleep."

Alex frowned. "Maybe he needs to get away for a while to sort things out. My family has a cabin standing empty in the mountains in Colorado. If he'd like, he's welcome to use it anytime."

"Ask him. I'm sure he'd love it. Getting out of St. Louis sounds like a wonderful idea," she added wistfully.

His gaze narrowed. "Your brother isn't the only one who sounds as though they could use a little R and R." Concern touched his voice. "How much sleep have you been getting lately?"

"Plenty," she said, trying to sound carefree and failing miserably. "If I look tired it's because I've been busy lately. I had to finish a large order of tassels for a local antique store. And with Christmas around the corner, I've got more orders coming in every day—"

"All of which you do at night when Jamie's in bed...after you've spent a full day teaching at school." Alex released an impatient breath. "Lindsey, you've got to slow down. Take care of yourself, for once."

"Alex, you worry too much." She smiled and tapped a finger on the jaw that he'd set in such a stubborn line. The beginnings of a late-day beard chafed her fingertip. "I'm fine, really."

He captured her hand and held it snug. "Somebody's got to worry about you. Obviously, you're too stubborn to think about yourself."

Her smile faded. His hand felt warm, strong, reassuring. She felt herself leaning toward him, overwhelmed by the temptation to rest her head against his wide shoulder and be embraced in the protective circle of his arms. These past two years had been difficult. There were times when she didn't know how she could carry on alone.

She'd be lying if she said it wouldn't feel good to have someone else to share the burden. But she could not allow herself the luxury. If these past few years had taught her anything, it was that she could depend on no one but her brother Rick, Jamie and herself.

The doorbell rang, announcing the arrival of more guests.

Lindsey slipped her hand from his, glad for the excuse to put some distance between them. "Alex, thank you for your concern." She forced a smile. "But right now, it's time for the party to begin."

Alex's expression remained grim.

She headed down the hall, not allowing herself to look

Chapter Two

Two hours later, the birthday boy finally ran out of steam. The guests, watching Jamie fall asleep as he ate his birthday cake and ice cream, took this as their cue to leave. Lindsey was exhausted by the time the last of Jamie's guests had said their goodbyes. Alex, Rick, and Sandy Martin, Lindsey's good friend and next door neighbor, lingered behind.

Sandy glanced around the messy kitchen and said, "Thank goodness my husband's already taken my kids home. I'll help you clean up before I leave."

"You don't have to," Lindsey said, stifling a yawn. "I can handle it myself."

"Right." Sandy chuckled. "And I'll be tucking you into bed right next to Jamie, if I don't. Goodness, Lindsey. I've never seen you looking so tired. You've got enough bags under your eyes for an entire set of luggage."

Lindsey rolled her eyes. "Really, Sandy—"

"Have you lost more weight?" Sandy narrowed a shrewd glance. "You look so thin."

Lindsey blushed. "Sandy, I'm fine."

"Fine, ha!" her friend snorted. "I bet dollars to doughnuts you've been spending more hours in your workroom making tassels than you have in your bed sleeping at night."

"Not you, too," Lindsey moaned.

Sandy frowned. "Me, too, what?"

"First, Alex. Now, you." She sighed. "Why's everyone so worried about my beauty sleep?"

"Maybe we wouldn't be so concerned if you weren't sleeping alone," Sandy said.

Trouble was brewing; Lindsey could see it as clearly as the devilish glint in her friend's eye. "Sandy—"

"Come on, Lindsey. You know I've been dying to ask you all night long...did you say yes?"

"Yes to what?" Alex asked as he walked into the kitchen carrying an armload of soiled napkins and paper plates.

"It—it's nothing," Lindsey said quickly, glaring at her friend.

"Nothing, ha! Lindsey's got a beau," Sandy announced. "He's asked her out on a date."

The paper plates clattered to the floor.

Rick stepped into the kitchen. "Jeez, Alex. You're making more of a mess than the kids did."

Alex shot him a prohibitive glance as he squatted to clean up the clutter.

"I think she should go for it," Sandy continued, oblivious to the dirty looks Lindsey was sending her way.

"Go for what?" Rick asked.

"A date, silly," Sandy said. "Don't you think it's

time Lindsey got back into the real world and started seeing men again?"

Rick shrugged. "Sure, why not?"

"Why not?" Lindsey gaped at her brother. He was the last person she expected to encourage her to start dating again. "I can think of a million reasons...Danny, being just one."

"Lindsey, you're a widow, not a nun. No one expects you to live like one," Rick said, slinging himself into one of the chairs at the kitchen table. "Danny's been gone for two years. If you're ready to start dating again, then do it."

Lindsey shut out the words of encouragement. They believed her to be a lonely widow, loyal to her husband's memory. They didn't know the truth. That it was guilt, not just loneliness that kept her awake at night.

"I don't know," Alex said slowly, breaking into her troubled thoughts. "Maybe it's not such a good idea for her to rush into any hasty decisions."

Heads turned, focusing curious gazes upon him.

He shifted uncomfortably beneath the attention. "Well? Does anybody know anything about this guy? For all we know he's a gigolo, preying on a vulnerable widow."

"He's not a gigolo, Alex," Sandy said with an amused smile. "He's an antique dealer. He owns two highly successful stores, one in Clayton and the other in Chesterfield. And he's a real dish to boot."

Lindsey closed her eyes and counted to ten, struggling to hold on to her temper. She couldn't believe that her brother and her friends were discussing her private life as though she weren't even in the room.

"Yeah, well, I still don't think she should rush things," Alex groused.

Eyebrows were raised in speculation.

Alex glanced around the room, scowling. "Hey, all I'm saying is, I know how it feels to be railroaded into a date by well-intentioned relatives."

Rick chuckled. "Sounds to me like Mama Trent's been putting a little pressure on the last of her unmarried children to settle down."

"A little pressure?" Alex shook his head. "The woman has the determination of a bulldog. She's been calling me every day with an updated list of single female guests who'll be attending my sister's wedding."

"So bring a date," Rick said.

"To a wedding? No, thank you. Do you have any idea how sentimental women get at weddings? They get all mushy and starry-eyed." Alex gave an exaggerated shudder. "The last thing I need to worry about is a matchmaking mother and a date who's under the influence of love, romance and a rose-colored view of marriage."

"Alex, really. You're incorrigible," Sandy said, her tone disgusted.

Lindsey watched the exchange in bemused silence, feeling an unsettling sense of disappointment. Alex's aversion to marriage shouldn't surprise her, she chided herself. For as long as she'd known him, he'd never shown any sign of being ready to settle down.

Why would she expect him to change now?

"Do you think we could change the subject?" Alex asked, drawing her out of her troubled thoughts. "It's Lindsey's personal life we were talking about, not mine. Maybe Lindsey isn't ready to start dating. Did anyone think to ask her?"

Heads turned again, this time focusing on Lindsey.

"Well?" Sandy demanded. "Are you ready to start dating, or not?"

Lindsey's cheeks warmed with embarrassment. "I think..." she stammered. "I think that I'd rather not have this conversation."

"Why not? Too afraid to admit you need more in life than coming home to an empty bed?" Sandy asked, smiling sweetly. "What's wrong with admitting you're a healthy adult, with normal, healthy needs and fantasies?"

"Fantasies?" Lindsey laughed out loud. "Who has the time? The closest thing I've come to having a fantasy is imagining myself alone on a tropical beach, with absolutely nothing to do except soak up some sun and drink an entire pitcher of margaritas."

"Sounds good to me," Rick quipped.

"You're missing the point, Rick," Lindsey growled.

Her brother frowned. "Which is?"

"The point is, that while I appreciate all of your concerns, I just don't have the time or the desire to pursue a relationship with a man." She gave a ragged sigh. "I'm just too darned tired to even consider it."

A thoughtful silence descended upon the room.

Sandy was the first to break it. "You know what I think?"

"No," Lindsey muttered. "But I'm sure you're going to tell me."

Sandy continued, undaunted by her grumpy tone. "I think what you really need is a vacation."

"A vacation?"

"That's right. And I have the perfect solution. You can go to Florida with Alex for his sister's wedding." She smiled, looking very pleased with the idea.

"Florida?" Lindsey repeated, staring dumbly at her friend. "I can't go to Florida with Alex."

"Why not?" Sandy demanded. "It'll solve both of your problems. Alex needs a date to keep his mother off his back. You need some R and R. It'll be perfect."

Lindsey felt the prickling unease of Alex watching her. Panic filled her chest, making it hard to breathe. While she considered Alex a good friend, whenever she saw him it was usually in the accompaniment of her brother, or with Jamie at her side. The thought of spending time alone with him unnerved her more than she cared to admit.

"It's out of the question," Lindsey insisted, refusing to meet Alex's gaze. "I have to work. You know...classes to teach, tassels to make."

"Next week is Thanksgiving. Doesn't your school go on break?" Sandy observed calmly.

"Thanksgiving!" Lindsey nearly shouted with relief. "I can't leave town on Thanksgiving. If I do, Rick won't have anywhere to go for his turkey dinner."

"Gee, thanks, brat," Rick drawled, looking amused. "But I don't think it'll kill me if I miss one Thanksgiving dinner."

"Fine, Rick may not need me. But my son does." Lindsey raised her chin, a picture of indignation. "What would I do with Jamie? I couldn't possibly leave him home all alone."

"Rick, you're welcome to join us for dinner, and Jamie can stay with me," Sandy offered. "You know he loves it at my house. He'll hardly notice you're gone."

"Thanks a lot," Lindsey said.

Alex, who'd been noticeably silent during the interchange, startled her by saying, "Lindsey, maybe you should give it some thought. Sandy's right. It'd be a solution to both of our problems. You need a break. And I definitely need someone to save me from my mother's good intentions.'' His warm smile melted her defenses. ''So what do you say? November in Florida may not be a tropical paradise, but it's the best I can offer on short notice.''

''Alex, I'm not sure…'' she said, wanting to kick herself for the vague-sounding answer.

''Come on, Lindsey,'' Alex persisted. ''You know I won't give up until you say yes.''

His blue eyes sparkled with a familiar determination. Work or play, Alex was a man who was used to getting his way. Lindsey knew she might as well give up the fight. Arguing with him would be pointless.

Besides, did she really want to argue with him?

Going away with Alex meant time away from all of her responsibilities. Time to relax. Time to do nothing but enjoy herself for an entire weekend.

She'd be crazy to say no.

Lindsey looked at Alex, taking in his handsome, determined face and his strong, supple body.

She'd be crazy to say yes.

She recalled the moment alone with Alex in the hallway, the temptation she'd felt when he had held her hand. Friend or not, Alex was an attractive man. Lately, she'd become more aware of this fact than ever before.

A new surge of panic tightened her chest, making it hard to breathe. The last thing she needed was to become entangled in an intimate relationship. Her marriage to Danny hadn't been a bed of roses. They had had their problems. She wasn't anxious to repeat her mistakes of the past.

''Lindsey,'' Alex said, his gentle tone softly persuading her to face him. ''We're friends, right?''

Friends—the word soothed her. Perhaps she was over-reacting. She'd known Alex for a long time. Not once in their relationship had he ever indicated he wanted more from her than friendship. Spending time alone with him would be as harmless as spending time alone with her brother. Right?

"Right," she said.

Encouraged, Alex continued. "Then, as friends, what's the harm in spending a few days together?"

What's the harm? She was sure there had to be at least a dozen potential dangers. But for the life of her, at the moment, she couldn't think of one of them. She sighed. "All right, Alex. I'll go with you to your sister's wedding."

"You won't regret this, Lindsey," he said.

Lindsey's heart thumped a warning beat as he blessed her with another irresistible smile.

She already did.

"I can't do this," Lindsey said, stopping midway to the doors of the airplane's loading gate.

Five days had passed since Jamie's birthday party. Five of the most trying days of his life. Alex bit back a groan. Getting Lindsey to agree to join him for his sister's wedding had been tough enough. Getting her on the plane was proving darned near impossible.

They were among the last to board. Fellow passengers skirted around them, sending them curious glances. Time was running out, and Lindsey was giving every indication of jumping ship.

"Now what's wrong," he said, not bothering to hide his impatience.

"Jamie," she said, her brown eyes wide and glistening. The tears looked ready to spill at any moment. "I've never left him before. He'll be devastated if I abandon him now. It will probably cause who knows what kind of damage to his psyche.''

They both glanced at the covey of plastic airport lounge chairs where they'd left Jamie in the care of Lindsey's friend, Sandy. The boy with the "damaged psyche" was busy pretending to be an airplane in flight, obviously not giving the departing adults a second thought.

"Yeah, he really looks like he's ready for the psychiatrist's chair," Alex mused.

Lindsey frowned. "He's just trying to be brave."

Jamie chose that moment to look at them. With a wave of his hand and a grin on his cherubic face, he sped off to join Sandy's oldest son, who had his nose pressed against the airport's glass-paneled walls, intent on watching a plane land on the runway.

A tear trickled down Lindsey's cheek. "I knew it. He's going to forget all about me."

"Lindsey," Alex said gently, whisking the tear away with the tips of his fingers. "Jamie's not going to forget about you. He's going to be fine."

She bit her lip to stop the trembling. "How can you be sure?"

"Because I just am." He captured her hand and led her toward the plane. "Now listen to me, Lindsey. Do you have any idea how lucky we were to get these tickets? It's the day before Thanksgiving. The busiest traveling day of the year. We'll never be able to get another flight."

She dragged her pump-clad feet, apparently not impressed by their good fortune.

"Just remember," he continued in his most soothing voice. "This is a vacation. You're not supposed to think about anything but relaxing. No Jamie. No Rick. No work." He gave a silent cheer of victory as they stepped onto the plane. "Nothing but the sand and the sea and taking it easy with me."

She stopped midaisle. "Rick? What am I thinking? He's going through an emotionally traumatic experience. He could lose his job. He shouldn't be alone at a time like this. He needs me."

A lesser man might have been miffed at the ease with which she'd brushed off the prospect of spending time alone with him on a tropical beach. Alex kept a firm grip on her hand, and his bruised ego.

"Lindsey, you're not going to help your brother if you're on the verge of burnout. You need this vacation. I'm not going to let you change your mind." He glanced over his shoulder at the doors being slammed shut. "Besides, it's too late. The plane's ready to take off."

"Take your seats, please," a flight attendant, a perky young blonde, said with a smile. "We're ready to depart."

"Oh, no," Lindsey moaned.

"Oh, yes," Alex said with a sigh of relief. He half led, half dragged her to their seats, giving her the window seat in hopes the view would take her mind off her misgivings.

He might have been hoping for a miracle.

"Do you have any idea how much work will be waiting for me when I get home?" she asked as she buckled her seat belt. A rhetorical question, obviously. She didn't bother waiting for an answer. "I'll be working twice as hard trying to fill all the orders before Christmas."

A new spill of tears threatened.

Alex sighed, again, feeling like hell for forcing her to go on this trip...even if it was for her own good. Getting her away from life's pressures—not to mention, the antique dealer who'd been hounding her for a date—was his top priority. It was the least he could do for the wife...that is, the widow, of his best friend, he assured himself.

He took her hand, giving it a gentle squeeze. "It'll be okay, Lindsey. Everything will be fine once we're in Florida."

The plane shimmied beneath their feet as it taxied along the runway.

She leaned against him, resting her head on his shoulder. "I'm sorry, Alex. I'm ruining your trip. I don't know what's the matter with me. I just feel so guilty."

"That's okay. You're a mom," he offered in way of explanation.

He brushed his chin against the top of her head. Her hair felt soft, tickling his skin. He breathed deeply, inhaling the scent of lavender and springtime; Lindsey's scent. The plane's engine surged as it lifted from the ground. Alex attributed the light buoyant feeling in the pit of his stomach to the effects of takeoff.

"What does being a mom have to do with feeling guilty?" she asked, sounding almost amused.

"Guilt's just part of the whole motherhood thing." He stroked his thumb across the palm of her hand. It felt soft, smooth, and all so delicate. He cleared his throat, struggling with an ill-timed surge of awareness. "When you're a mom, you feel as though you have to take care of everyone else. I speak from experience, mind you. My mother's the world's most notorious worrier. Your nurturing instincts kick into overdrive when you're a mother. It's going to take a while before they downshift into neutral."

She sighed. "I suppose you're right."

"Of course I am." His grin was devilish. "Aren't I always?"

She angled her face upward to look at him and, for the first time that day, she smiled. "Oh, Alex. What would I do without you?"

Emotion stuck in his throat, making it impossible to answer. Another rhetorical question, thank goodness. Because it was one question that she need not ever ask. They both knew he would always be there for her.

With a contented sigh, she snuggled against him, the tension melting from her body.

Alex, on the other hand, suddenly felt as taut as a drum.

One look into her trusting, innocent eyes and his protective instincts had been put on full alert. Yet the feel of her soft curves pressed against him had his blood pumping hot and thick. An undeniable awareness pulsed through his veins. To complicate matters further, guilt was stretching its icy fingers deep inside him, chilling him to the bone. He felt hot, cold and tense all at the same time. Alex gave a silent moan. Lindsey was slowly, ever so slowly, sending him into sensory overload.

What the hell was wrong with him? he chided himself. Lindsey needed a chance to relax, to unwind. She didn't need to be lusted after by someone she trusted, someone she considered a *friend*.

But, then again, he'd be lying if he didn't admit he'd always thought of Lindsey as a beautiful woman. It felt so good, so right, holding her close, touching her. For just a moment he allowed himself to imagine what it would be like if the circumstances were different, if she weren't the widow of his best friend, if they were alone without another soul in sight...

Thump-thump-thump.

Alex nearly jumped out of his seat at the noise, sure the plane was about to crash. A just punishment for him and his prurient thoughts, he told himself.

The thumping noise stopped as the flight attendant rolled the drink cart up to their seats.

"First time flying?" she asked, glancing at Lindsey's tear-stained face. She flashed a smile at Alex. "Perhaps your wife would like a drink to calm her nerves?"

"Wife?" Alex stiffened. Instant heat suffused his face.

Lindsey lifted her head off his shoulder so quick Alex feared she'd suffer from whiplash. She snatched her hand from his and blurted a hasty denial. "I'm not his wife."

"No, of course not. We're friends," Alex said, feeling the totally inappropriate need to explain. "Just good friends."

Lindsey brought a hand to her throat. Her wedding ring, the ring Danny had given her, glinted in the overhead light. "We're traveling together."

"To attend my sister's wedding," Alex added, speaking around the lump of guilt lodged in his throat.

"I see," the attendant said, volleying a wary glance between the two of them. "Well, then, would your 'friend' care for a drink?"

Alex looked at Lindsey. Her face had turned about two shades pinker in the last few seconds. She shook her head, refusing to meet his gaze.

Alex cleared his throat. "No, thank you."

The attendant nodded. "Perhaps later..."

Alex smiled wanly.

The attendant left them then, pushing her cart down the aisle.

An uncomfortable silence stretched between them.

Lindsey shifted in her seat, tugging at the hem of her rust-colored skirt. Alex watched as she scooted herself as far away from him as the narrow seats would allow. New lines of tension etched her face. All of the progress he'd made toward easing her worries were for naught. She looked as uncomfortable now as she had before she'd boarded the plane. Lindsey glanced at her watch and feigned a yawn.

"Would you look at the time. It's already three o'clock. I had to get up early this morning to pack, then off to school…well, I'm just exhausted. You don't mind if I take a nap, do you?"

"No, of course not," he said quickly.

Without another word, she folded her jacket into a pillow, curled her body away from him, and squeezed her eyes shut.

Alex felt like an idiot.

An unexpected anger simmered deep inside him, threatening to bubble out of control. Not an anger directed at Lindsey, for she'd done nothing wrong, but at himself. He was the one who'd broken the terms of their friendship. Holding her close, comforting her was an indulgence he should never have allowed.

He'd had no right.

The only man who had that right was his best friend. A man who'd been dead for nearly two years. A man Lindsey had, obviously, never stopped loving.

Chapter Three

"Lindsey," a familiar, teasing voice whispered, rousing her from her nap. "Rise and shine, sleepyhead. We're ready to land."

She took her time waking up. With a purr of contentment, she allowed herself a luxuriant stretch—at least, as luxuriant as possible in the tiny seat—working the kinks out of her body. Her arm brushed against a masculine shoulder, sending goose bumps of awareness skittering up her limb.

Her eyes flew open.

Tentatively, Alex met her gaze.

In a heartbeat, the reason for her escape into slumberland came back to her with the force of a blow. She'd practically thrown herself into Alex's arms. The flight attendant had believed them to be married. The mistake had embarrassed Alex. She'd seen that as clearly as the blush on his cheeks.

Now, he was looking at her with such uncertainty it made her heart ache with regret.

The plane bumped to a stop, throwing her off kilter. Passengers stood, gathering their belongings. Alex rose to his feet. Lindsey followed at a slower pace, giving herself a moment to recover her balance.

He stepped into the aisle, waiting for her to join him. His hand pressed lightly against the small of her back, guiding her as she moved into the aisle. The gesture sent tingles along her spine. It felt too intimate, reminding her too clearly of the stirring sensation that being close to him earlier had caused in the pit of her stomach.

Lindsey bit back a moan. Agreeing to this vacation with Alex had been a mistake. She felt unbalanced. Her emotions were too close to the surface. Who knew what might happen when she was in such a confused state?

An hour passed by the time they gathered their bags and paid for a rental car. It was dark when they stepped outside. The air felt warm, moist against her skin. In St. Louis, it had been thirty degrees. Here, in Florida, the temperature hovered in the sixties. Her sweater and wool skirt felt heavy and uncomfortable. She longed to change into something cooler.

Obviously, Alex felt the same way. He loaded their bags into the trunk. Then, with a grunt of satisfaction, he stripped out of his suit jacket, tossing it onto the back seat before he started the car. His tie quickly followed.

"Comfy?" she asked with an amused smile.

He grinned.

"Hey, it's a vacation, remember?"

Lindsey relaxed at his teasing tone, feeling as though they were regaining the footing of their old friendship.

Alex drove confidently through the night-darkened streets. It was seven o'clock, St. Louis time—eight o'clock in Florida. The traffic was light, the streets dark and glistening from an earlier rain. Lindsey sat back and enjoyed the ride.

His parents lived in a beachside estate on Whisper Key, one of the many islands that dappled the Gulf coastline of Florida. Their white stucco house was large and luxurious. As soon as they pulled into the circle drive, Lindsey was struck with a sharp reminder of the differences between her and Alex's backgrounds.

She'd grown up the daughter of a St. Louis policeman. Until her marriage to Danny, she'd lived with her father in a two-family flat in south St. Louis. By no stretch of the imagination could she have considered her family wealthy. But they were rich in other ways, love being just one of those.

Alex, on the other hand, grew up in a palatial home in Ladue. It was only after his graduation from college that his parents had moved to Florida. He was born with the proverbial silver spoon in his mouth, never wanting for anything. Despite his family's affluence, he was the most unassuming man she'd ever met.

Alex and his brother worked hard building their own company. For them, money was an afterthought, not a constant worry. Success seemed to be their main goal. Sometimes it was easy for her to forget that they came from such differing backgrounds.

"Relax," he said as he helped her from the car. "My parents know you're coming. They've promised to be on their best behavior."

"Your parents," Lindsey murmured thoughtfully.

Alex disappeared around the back of the car to unload their bags from the trunk.

Frowning, she followed him, asking, "Alex, exactly what did you tell them about...well, about my coming with you?"

He shrugged. "Just that you were looking forward to some time away from St. Louis."

"Yes, but—"

She never had a chance to finish. The front door flew open and a tawny-haired young woman raced down the stairs toward them. Before Alex could say hello, she threw herself into his arms.

"Alex! I can't believe you're finally here."

"Hey, sis," Alex chuckled as he hauled the woman into a bear hug. "It's good to see you, too."

"Why didn't you call when you got in?" she demanded when her toes were once again touching the ground. Graceful and fit, blond and beautiful, she reminded Lindsey of a feminine version of Alex. The Trent family resemblance was unmistakable. "I would have picked you up at the airport."

He tugged on a strand of blond hair. "I didn't want to bother you. Besides, I'll need a car while I'm here." He caught Lindsey's curious gaze. "Lindsey, I don't know if you've ever met my sister. Stephanie, this is Lindsey, Rick's sister."

"Rick's sister, eh?" Stephanie raised a brow. Then, with a mischievous glint in her eyes, she extended a hand and said, "I promise not to hold it against you."

Lindsey stared at her, uncertain what to say.

"Ignore her, Lindsey," Alex said, looking amused. "She remembers Rick from when she was in junior high. He used to pull her ponytail and call her brat."

"Well, in that case, you have my fullest empathy. He calls me by that awful nickname, too," Lindsey said, accepting the proffered hand.

"Stephanie, Alex, where are your manners? Stop chattering and bring our guest inside," an older woman scolded from the doorway.

"Yes, Mother," Alex and Stephanie chorused, cha-
grined looks on their faces.

Alex slammed the trunk lid, startling her. Lindsey
jumped, uncertain why she should suddenly feel ill at
ease. It wasn't until Alex rested a reassuring hand on
her shoulder that she forced herself to move.

His mother was a petite woman. Her silvery-blond
hair had faded slightly with age. Her face was kind and
beautiful. It was easy to see where Alex had gotten his
good looks. After giving her son a hug and a fond buss
on the cheek, she turned her attention to Lindsey. She
seemed inordinately pleased by her presence.

"I'm so glad you could come, my dear," she said,
taking Lindsey by the arm, speaking gently as she led
her up a stairway of marble. "Have you eaten dinner,
yet?"

"Um—no," Lindsey said, trying not to ogle the
house's rich furnishings. "But I'm really not that hungry."

With the walls painted white and the windows placed
with an optimum view of the ocean in mind, the house
had a light, airy feel about it. It was large and spacious,
with an eclectic mix of contemporary and traditional furnishings. Yet it had a comfortable, lived-in quality. It
was a place where anyone could feel at home.

"Well, perhaps you'd like a sandwich later. Right
now, I'll show you to your rooms. I thought you and
Alex might like to freshen up after your trip."

"Thank you, that would be wonderful," Lindsey said,
glancing back at Alex. He followed behind, deep in a
conversation with his sister.

"I do hope you'll enjoy your visit," Mrs. Trent continued. "I was so pleased when Alex called to say you
were coming."

"Thank you," Lindsey repeated, wondering what else Alex might have mentioned about her. Since Jamie's birthday party, they hadn't discussed the details of her role in this weekend's festivities. As far as she knew, Alex might still be expecting her to play the part of his "girlfriend."

Soon his mother opened a door off the long hall. "This room's for you, Alex," she called over her shoulder. She stepped down the hall to room the next door. "And this is yours, Lindsey."

The room was painted a pale yellow. Its furnishings were contemporary and comfortable. A delicate, creamy-eyelet spread covered the bed. The curtains were pulled back, revealing a veranda with a breathtaking view of the Gulf.

A door opened. Alex walked in, carrying her bags. He raised a questioning brow. "Where do you want me to put your things?"

Lindsey stared at him, too stunned to speak.

Alex hadn't entered from the hall door. But rather from a side door opening directly into her bedroom. Which could mean only one thing. His mother had given them adjoining rooms!

"I—I, uh…" Lindsey stammered, feeling the heat rise on her face.

Alex's sister stood in the doorway, watching the scene with bemused interest.

Mrs. Trent beamed with satisfaction. "Well, we'll just let you settle in. Whenever you're ready, come downstairs and I'll make you a bite to eat." She grabbed Stephanie by the arm and pulled her from the room. "Come along, Stephanie. Time for these two to be alone."

The door closed behind the pair, leaving Lindsey to stare numbly at Alex.

An unusually quiet Alex dropped the bags on the floor, beating a hasty retreat out the door through which he'd first appeared.

"Alex," she said, her voice a strangled note.

He stopped, turning slowly to look at her.

"What did you tell your mother?" she demanded. "About me? About us?"

He shrugged. "Just that we were friends."

"She thinks we're more than friends, Alex." Lindsey noted that the pitch of her voice rose with each word she spoke. Loud enough that others might hear. But, at this point, she just didn't care. "Your mother has given us adjoining rooms."

He had the grace to look sheepish. "Look, Lindsey. My mother may have gotten the wrong impression—"

"Wrong impression? She's assuming we make it a habit of sharing bedrooms!" she hollered.

"Lindsey, calm down," he said, his tone irritatingly reasonable. "I know what Sandy suggested—that you should pretend to be my date for the weekend—but trust me, Lindsey. I couldn't...I wouldn't use you that way. I told my mother we were just friends. Any conclusions she might have drawn to the contrary are of her own imaginings."

Lindsey crossed her arms and narrowed a shrewd glance at him. "You don't seem too surprised by all this, Alex. Why do I get the impression you already knew about your mother's *conclusions?*"

He hesitated.

"Alex—" she said, her tone a warning note. She waited, tapping an impatient foot. A useless gesture. The plush carpeting swallowed up the angry beat.

He fingered the collar of his button-down shirt. "My mother may have mentioned something to the effect that she believed us to be—" he swallowed hard "—involved."

"And you didn't bother to try to clear up the misunderstanding?"

He sighed. "Lindsey, I tried. But you've got to understand my mother. Once she's set her mind on something, it would take a bulldozer to budge it."

She stared at him, her gaze incredulous. "So I'm supposed to go on letting your mother think we're involved...intimately."

"It's only a few days, Lindsey."

"Alex—"

"Once the wedding's over you won't have to worry about what my mother thinks."

She shook her head. "I can't do that. Your mother's so sweet. I hate the thought of deceiving her."

"You can't deceive someone if you've never lied to them in the first place," he said, his tone annoyingly matter-of-fact.

She stared at him for a moment, taking in his boyishly innocent expression, his handsome face.

"Tell me the truth, Alex. This misunderstanding doesn't bother you nearly as much as it bothers me. As long as your mother believes you to be involved with me, she won't try playing matchmaker during the wedding festivities, will she?"

"Well..." He shifted uncomfortably, averting his gaze.

"The truth is, despite all protests to the contrary, you really are using me, Alex."

"Never." He looked at her, his eyes wide, his gaze

sincere. "I'd never do anything to hurt you, Lindsey. You know that."

She didn't answer.

Her silence shook him; she could see that by the glint of emotion in his eye. He took a determined step for the door. "I'll talk to my mother, right now. There are plenty of rooms in this house. I'm sure she can find you a room with more privacy."

"Alex," she said, stopping him. She took a deep breath, swallowing the last of her anger. "It's okay. This room will be fine."

He frowned. "Are you sure?"

"Positive."

"What about my mother?"

Lindsey sighed. "I'm sure she'll figure out the truth, sooner or later. All she has to do is look at us to know there's nothing between us but a friendship. Right?"

"Right," he said, hesitating only a moment.

The pause wasn't long. Just enough to send second thoughts skittering through her mind. She pushed aside her lingering doubts and stooped to picked up her bag. In a cool voice, she said, "I'd like to change before we eat."

He nodded reluctantly, looking as though he'd like to say more. Without another word, however, he moved to the door, closing it quietly behind him.

Lindsey fought the urge to lock the door that stood between them. Now, more than ever, she had to rely on her instincts. Her instincts were telling her that she could trust Alex.

Trusting herself...now that was a whole other matter.

Twenty minutes later Alex knocked softly on Lindsey's door. There was no answer.

Panic gripped him, setting his heart thumping against his chest. He recalled the hurt look in Lindsey's eye, the disappointed expression on her face when he'd tried to explain about the misunderstanding with his mother. She'd been angry. Surely she wouldn't have left without telling him.

He knocked again, harder this time.

Still, no answer.

Not giving himself time to reconsider, he opened the door. The room was quiet, except for the sound of the surf hitting the beach outside. The curtain fluttered at the French doors. A soft breeze filtered in from the veranda, scenting the air with a salty tang.

Alex strode to the veranda.

She stood at the railing, looking out upon the night-darkened water.

Alex breathed a quiet sigh of relief. Thank God, she hadn't left.

She'd changed her clothes. Now, she wore a pale blue, short-sleeved sweater and a long, flowing, blue print skirt. Lifting her face to the heavens, her hair loose and dancing in the wind, she looked contented, at peace with the world. He'd never seen her looking more beautiful…or more desirable.

Slowly, hesitantly, he approached her. His heel scuffed the concrete floor, making a scraping noise.

She wheeled around, smiling a greeting.

And Alex's heart lurched in his chest.

For the first time in his memory, he'd lied to her…earlier, when he'd agreed that all one had to do was look at them to see that there was nothing between them but friendship. Something was definitely happening between them.

A change.

A forbidden attraction.

An age-old awareness between a man and a woman. At least, on his part.

"It's so peaceful here," she said finally.

He forced himself to move. He joined her, leaning a hip against the balustrade. "Still glad you came?"

"Yes, I'm still glad." She looked out at the sea, inhaling deeply. Her breasts rose and fell with each breath. "This is the first time I've taken time out for myself since Danny died."

An arrow of guilt pierced his heart at the mention of his friend. He struggled with the emotion.

"I've been so busy working and taking care of Jamie, I'd almost forgotten who I am. Maybe I'll find myself again this weekend," she said, her tone wistful.

"Maybe I could help you look?" he offered.

She glanced at him.

Their gazes held for a long moment.

He wasn't sure if she understood that he was talking about more than a journey into self-awareness. He was talking about a reawakening...of the romantic kind. Alex felt himself leaning toward her, fighting the urge to reach out and touch her. Whether it be a trick of the moonlight, or wishful thinking on his part, he swore the desire he felt was mirrored in her beautiful, dark eyes. He couldn't help but wonder if she was tempted by his offer.

She drew in a sharp breath, exhaling slowly. A quick, polite smile followed. "Thank you, Alex. But I think this is something I'll have to handle myself."

Obviously he'd been mistaken. The lady wasn't interested in anything he had to offer. To Lindsey, he would always be Danny's friend. He would always be her friend, nothing more. He tried not to let his disappointment show. Forcing a light tone, he said, "I don't know about you, but I'm starved. What do you say? Ready to raid my mother's refrigerator?"

Her tummy growled in response. She laughed, a light, melodious sound on the night air. "More than ready."

Resting a hand on her shoulder, he followed her back inside. The delicate balance of their friendship nearly recovered. The intimacy of the moment almost forgotten.

Except his heart still pounded like a jackhammer in his chest. His body still thrummed with a lusty need that had nothing to do with food. And his mind still raced with a yearning he couldn't quite erase.

Chapter Four

Her room was aglow with light by the time she opened her eyes the next morning. But it wasn't the sunshine that had awakened her. It was the pounding on her door...the door adjoining her bedroom to Alex's.

"Wake up, Lindsey." Alex's voice filtered in through the wood-paneled door.

"Go away, Alex," she moaned, pulling the covers over her head.

"Come on, honey. The sun's shining. It's gotta be over seventy degrees out there already. We're wasting valuable time that we could be spending outside."

Lindsey poked her nose out of the covers far enough to squint at her alarm clock. Eleven o'clock. She blinked, then looked again. Yep, it was really eleven o'clock. She couldn't remember the last time she'd slept this late.

Stretching lazily, she tossed the covers aside and pushed herself out of bed. She jammed her feet into her slippers and scuffled across the room. Yawning widely, she threw open the door.

Alex stood leaning an arm against the doorjamb. Wordlessly, he scanned her body, taking in the oversize T-shirt and the pink fuzzy slippers. A wicked grin touched his lips. "Did anyone ever tell you you look like hell in the morning?"

Lindsey eyed him with a scowl. She certainly couldn't say the same for Alex. Wearing a loose-fitting shirt and swimming trunks, he looked especially nice this morning. She caught a glimpse of his long, powerful legs, his lean, flat stomach and his strong, wide shoulders. Lindsey gave a silent sigh of appreciation. Years of running had certainly paid off where Alex's physique was concerned. She was almost tempted to take up the sport.

She pushed a disheveled lock of hair out of her eyes. "Did you wake me up just to tell me that?"

"Nope, I woke you up to see if you wanted to stretch your legs, get a little exercise on the beach." He glanced at the legs in question.

Reflexively, Lindsey tugged at the hem of her T-shirt. Moments ago, it had seemed modest enough, its length reaching past her thighs. Now, under his blue-eyed scrutiny, the shirt seemed woefully inadequate.

His words filtered into her sleep-fogged brain, sending a protest throughout her body. Alex was an avid jogger. On a given day, he ran anywhere from three to five miles.

"Alex, you know I don't run. I'd never be able to keep up with you."

His smile deepened. "That's okay, Lindsey. I was thinking of a picnic on the beach and maybe a walk afterward. Or if you're feeling especially brave, a dip in the Gulf."

She bit her lip, feeling tempted. "What about your

"But your mother, what will she think—"

"My mother's the one who suggested the picnic on
the beach. She's making up a basket as we speak."

Lindsey gave up the protests. "All right, Alex. I'll be
ready in five minutes."

Shutting the door, she stripped off her T-shirt and
headed for the dresser where she'd stowed her clothes
last night. In the top drawer she found the swimsuit that
she'd bought before leaving St. Louis. It was white, one-
pieced and maillot-styled. A little too high-cut in the legs
and a little too low-cut in the neckline for her taste, but
considering it was off-season and there wasn't much of
a selection in the stores, it would have to do.

Pushing aside her doubts, she stepped into the suit and
slid on a pair of shorts to cover the high-cut legs. After
brushing her teeth, running a comb through her hair and
adding a light touch of makeup, five minutes later on
the button, she stood on the veranda, waiting for Alex.

He joined her moments later, toting a picnic basket.
He grinned. "I can't believe it. A woman who's actually
ready on time."

She tilted her nose in the air disdainfully. "I take that
as an insult to all of womankind, Alex Trent. Perhaps, I
won't join you on the beach, after all."

"Too bad, you're going to miss a great lunch," he
said unconcernedly. He lifted a corner of the basket lid.
"Let's see, there's all kinds of cheese and sausages, lots

of fancy crackers, some fruit and…ah, yes, cheesecake for dessert.''

"You make it hard for a girl to say no," Lindsey groaned, rubbing her empty stomach.

"Just a negotiating technique I've picked up at work," he said with the assurance of a man who'd had years of experience. "Find an opponent's weakness and use it to make them an offer they can't refuse." He tapped a finger on the tip of her nose. "And you, my dear, have yet to turn down a meal."

"Alex, you're terrible," she said, swatting away his hand and relaxing beneath the lighthearted banter, glad that last night's tension seemed to have melted beneath the heat of daylight. She followed him down the veranda steps. The porch emptied directly onto the beach. Her feet sank into soft, white sand. She slipped off her sandals and buried her toes into the cool sand. "Jamie would love this. A whole backyard that's just one big sandbox.''

Alex chuckled. "Remind me to bring him along the next time we come.''

Next time?

As in, there'd be another?

Lindsey dared not comment. She brushed off the remark as a casual promise, one a person would make without really meaning it. After all, what possible reason would Alex have in bringing her back here again?

"Where to?" she asked, surveying the wide-open beach. Other than the seagulls dancing in the sky overhead, and the waves lapping at the shore, they were alone on the beach.

"Anywhere you want," he said, his tone unassuming. "It's a private beach."

"A private beach, eh?" She raised a speculative brow.

"You know, Alex, this vacation is starting to sound more and more like my fantasy every minute. All I need is a pitcher of margaritas and I'd be all set."

He snapped his fingers. "How could I forget? Give me a minute, and I'll see what I can do." He made a move toward the house.

She put a hand on his arm, stopping him. His skin felt warm, kissed by the sun. Her fingers sizzled at the contact.

He looked at her, a question in his eyes.

She licked her lips nervously. "Alex, I was just teasing. You've got to stop pampering me. I'm going to be so spoiled by the time I get back to St. Louis, I'll be terrible to live with."

"Impossible," he said with such sincerity it nearly took her breath away. "After everything you've been through these past couple of years, you deserve a little pampering. My only regret is that I only have three days to spoil you."

Lindsey found it impossible to look away. She allowed herself to be held by his gaze longer than it was wise. Each passing second seemed like an eternity. Warning signals erupted deep inside her. Alex was a charmer. Countless women had fallen under his spell to prove that much. If she wasn't careful, she'd be the next in line to take the tumble. Her stomach fluttered with confusion by the time she forced herself to break the contact.

She pointed to a strip of sand that was dry and relatively flat. "How about over there? That looks like a good place to eat."

Alex nodded a silent agreement.

His mother had thoughtfully packed a blanket for them to stretch out on. Within minutes, they had the food spread on the blanket and were demolishing the contents of the basket.

By the time Lindsey licked the last crumb of cheesecake from her fingers, a sated, contented feeling wafted over her. She leaned back and watched a seagull swoop down over the water, diving for his own lunch. "I wonder how Jamie slept last night."

"He must have done okay, or we'd have heard from Sandy."

"He should be having his turkey dinner soon. Sandy said their family would be eating at noon."

Alex gave her a sideways glance. "Am I detecting a bit of melancholy in your tone?"

She grinned sheepishly. "Not exactly. I just miss Jamie. It's the first time we've been apart overnight."

"He'll be fine. Sandy's a good mom. She's not going to let anything bad happen to Jamie."

"I know, I know…it's just hard not to worry about him."

Alex gathered up the plates and napkins and began stuffing them into the basket. "Idle hands make idle minds." He frowned. "At least, I think that's how the saying goes. My mother said it often enough when we were kids. Anyway, the point is, we need to keep you busy, Lindsey. Or the next thing I know, you'll start blubbering again, just like you did on the plane."

She raised her chin indignantly. "I wasn't blubbering—"

"Lindsey," he interrupted. "If it'll make you feel better, of course you can call Jamie later, before we eat dinner. But for now, why don't we try enjoying ourselves? What do you say, ready for that walk?"

"More than ready." She started to rise.

Alex hesitated, frowning as he studied her body from

head to toe. "Maybe you'd better put some sunscreen on first. You're starting to get a little pink around the edges."

She promptly flushed a deeper hue beneath the intensity of his scrutiny. "I didn't think to bring anything…"

He dug into the basket and pulled out a tube of lotion. "No problem. My mother thinks of everything."

Her fingers brushed his as she took the tube from his hand. Ignoring the goose bumps, she slathered on the lotion. She made good progress, despite the fact that Alex was a captivated audience, until she reached her back. Swallowing hard, she looked at Alex.

He raised a brow. "Need some help?"

His expression was so innocent, so guileless, how could she say no? She handed him the lotion.

He poured a dollop onto his hands, rubbing them together to warm the lotion before he touched her. But when he did…Lindsey nearly jumped off the blanket at the contact. Her stomach did a flip-flop as he smoothed his strong hands over her back. From her shoulders to the small of her back, not an inch of skin was left unattended. She sat stiffly on the blanket, too afraid to move, as she endured his ministrations. The ordeal felt perfectly, awfully…wonderful.

"Well, that about covers it," Alex said, his voice sounding strange and forced. His breathing seemed ragged, as though he'd just ran a mile at a fast clip.

She swung around to look at him.

He stood, quickly, averting his gaze. He busied himself with repacking the basket.

With a frown, Lindsey followed his lead, pretending nothing was wrong. Rising to her feet, she shook out the blanket and refolded it. She held it out to Alex to repack.

He took the blanket, still without meeting her gaze.

Lindsey rolled her eyes. Goodness, this would never work. They couldn't spend a day together without making eye contact. "Is there something wrong, Alex?"

"Wrong?" he said gruffly as he squatted and stuffed the blanket into the basket. "What could be wrong?"

"I don't know. You tell me. You're the one who won't look at me."

Releasing a slow, whistling breath, he lifted his eyes to meet hers. There was something different in his gaze, an awareness that hadn't been there before. He knew she'd been affected by the intimacy of his touch.

They'd reached a turning point in their relationship. One that she'd hoped to deny. For the past two years, she'd lived a life of virtual seclusion, ignoring her own needs and desires. It would be so easy to give in to her wants, to hang the consequences and let Alex show her all the things that had been missing in her life.

And then what?

Alex didn't have a committal bone in his body. He went through women like they were tissues in a box, tossing them aside one right after another. She wasn't foolish enough to believe she could be the woman to change his errant ways. Her hormones may be ready to take the risk, but her heart just wasn't up to the task.

There were more important things to consider, besides her libido. Jamie, for one. Alex was an important part of his life. She'd never do anything to jeopardize their relationship. And, perhaps on a more selfish note, she'd grown accustomed to Alex's presence in her own life. Since Danny's death, he'd become her confidant, her comic relief, her Rock of Gibraltar.

He'd become one of her best friends.

"You know what I think?" she said slowly.

He didn't answer.

"I think...that you ate too much of your mother's picnic lunch, and now you're too full and too grumpy to take that walk you promised me."

He narrowed his gaze. "Is that right?"

"Uh-huh," she said, forcing a light tone. "I saw that double helping of cheesecake you scoffed down. Now you're just embarrassed. Too afraid to admit that you won't be able to keep up with me."

"Keep up with you?" He feigned indignation, but she saw the smile struggling to surface. "I've never heard of anything so ridiculous—"

She breathed a quiet sigh of relief. They were skirting a fine line between friendship and desire. For the moment, they'd avoided crossing the boundary. She had every intention of seeing to it that their relationship remained unchanged throughout the remainder of their vacation.

"Oh, yeah?" She backstepped, sending him a challenging look. "Prove it!"

Without a backward glance, she turned and sprinted barefoot across the beach, confident he would follow. Seashells poked out of the sand, pricking her soles and slowing her down. He caught up with her before she'd gone even a few feet.

"Too full, eh? Too tired?" Grabbing her around her waist, he slung her up into his arms. With Lindsey in tow, he headed for the water's edge. "Let's just see who's grumpy after they've taken a swim."

"Put me down, Alex," Lindsey demanded, kicking her feet and laughing at the same time.

Grinning wickedly, he ignored her protest.

Water foamed around his ankles, then his knees, and still he did not stop. By the time he was thigh-deep, panic set in. Lindsey was clinging to him like a life-jacket. She'd quickly changed her tune. "Alex, don't you dare drop me."

"What's that, Lindsey?" he chided. "Where's your sense of adventure?"

"It's almost winter, Alex. The water's got to be freezing," she pleaded. "I'm too old to survive the shock cold water will have on my system."

"Old? Lindsey, you're only twenty-five," he reminded her. He moved ahead, undaunted by her dire predictions. Soon, icy cold water lapped at her dangling feet, tickling her derriere.

Lindsey squealed a protest. "Alex, you'll pay dearly if you drop me now."

Her threat bounced right off of him. His smile deepened. "Sue away, darling. It'll be worth the price."

"I knew it all along," she said primly. "You are a man with too much money and too little morals."

He shook his head. "Lindsey, you just don't know when to keep your mouth shut, do you?"

With that, he released her.

Lindsey tumbled into the water. The tide pulled her under, completely immersing her with an icy bath. The shock stole her breath away. Sputtering and coughing, she thrashed her hands and feet, struggling to find a foothold.

Within seconds a pair of strong hands grabbed her by the waistband of her shorts and hauled her to the surface. She heard the laughter in his voice as he asked, "Ready to admit you were wrong?"

"Not on your life, buster," she choked, flailing her arms in a vain attempt to strike out at him.

She felt herself being lowered back into the water. She squealed another protest. "All right, Alex. I'll admit, you're not the weakling I believed you to be."

"That's more like it," he growled. He set her on her feet, his hands lingering at her waist to steady her.

Shivering, Lindsey fought the urge to smack him on his smug face. She'd learned her lesson. She didn't need another dip in the frigid water. "That was a crummy thing to do, Alex."

"You're the one who started it."

She stuck out her lower lip, feeling peevish and out of sorts. "Yeah, well, you don't play fair."

"All's fair in love—" his voice caught "—and war."

How could such a familiar saying have such a devastating effect? Suddenly she was all too aware of his hands at her waist, steadying her. Only, she didn't feel steady. She felt dizzy and out of control.

It wouldn't take much, mere inches, to close the gap between them. A hairbreadth of distance to stand on tiptoe and sample his tempting lips. She had a feeling they'd taste better than any decadent dessert.

With a long shiver, she pushed herself out of his arms. "It's cold," she said in way of explanation as she headed for the shore.

Water splashed behind her, telling her Alex was following.

She didn't look back until she reached the abandoned picnic basket. She sat on the sand, tucking her knees beneath her chin, willing the sun to work its magic on her frozen limbs. Even though she knew the cold that had her quivering was from deep within her heart, not from an external source.

Alex sat next to her, remaining quiet for a moment. Then, with a sigh, he asked, "What do you want to do now?"

She shrugged an answer.

"We could finish that walk. Or if you'd rather, we

could swim in the pool by the house. It won't be as private. My family will probably be hanging around and bothering us, but it is heated.''

"Sounds good to me," she said quickly. At the moment, being surrounded by other people sounded like the best course of action. She didn't trust herself to be alone with Alex.

He stood, reaching out a hand to help her to her feet. Lindsey bit her lip, hesitating.

He blew out an impatient breath. "I'm just trying to be nice, Lindsey. I promise I won't throw you back into the water...no matter how much I might want to.''

She looked up at him, startled. He was grinning, looking once again like the familiar, teasing Alex she'd come to know and depend on. Slowly, she returned his smile. Then accepted his proffered hand.

She couldn't deny the trembling of awareness that the contact provoked. But she dropped her hand quickly, determined not to let her traitorous body give her away. The truth was, she decided, she'd been without a man in her life too long. She ached with an unfulfilled need.

The problem was, as confusing as the realization might be, it seemed Alex was the man she wanted to fulfill that need.

The problem was...he'd never wanted a woman as much as he did Lindsey.

Moodily, Alex watched as she dove into the water, arms outstretched, her legs, then toes, disappearing beneath the surface of the pool. She'd shucked off the shorts hours ago, leaving her legs bare and beautiful. The sunshine was turning her long limbs a golden hue.

It had been months, possibly years, since she looked

so relaxed, so vibrant. Bringing Lindsey to Florida was doing wonders for her health and well-being.

However, it was wreaking havoc on his peace of mind.

He couldn't look at her without wanting her. But as quickly as it arose, desire was extinguished by the cooling effects of guilt. Guilt because Lindsey wasn't like any other woman he knew. She was innocent, beautiful and vulnerable. And if Danny were still alive, he'd have his hide for the thoughts passing through his mind. Alex gave a ragged sigh. Hell, who was he kidding? He'd been having those thoughts about Lindsey even before Danny died. That was the real reason why he couldn't shake the guilt.

A shadow fell across his lounge chair. Alex glanced up to find his brother, Jon, standing in front of him, a quizzical expression on his face.

"It's about time you showed up," Alex groused. "Mom's been driving us crazy, fretting all day over whether you'd be late for Thanksgiving dinner."

Jon slung himself onto the chair next to Alex's. "It couldn't be helped. Something came up."

"With work?" Alex frowned. "Everything go okay in California?"

"Business is fine, little brother. The problem's strictly personal." Jon raised his sunglasses, squinting at the lithe figure gliding through the pool. Lindsey surfaced, flipping over to float on her back. "Holy cow, is that who I think it is?" He looked at Alex, his expression amused. "You brought Lindsey to the wedding?"

"Yes, I brought Lindsey," Alex growled. "She's been under a lot of stress lately. She needed a vacation. I invited her to join me for the weekend. She accepted. End of story. We're just friends, nothing more."

"This is your brother you're talking to," Jon said, settling himself more comfortably into his seat. "You may have everyone else fooled with that 'just friends' bit, but not me. I know you've been half in love with Lindsey since the day you met her."

"You're crazy, too," Alex said, keeping an eye on Lindsey's approaching form. He lowered his voice. "Lindsey married Danny long after I met her."

"Doesn't stop a man from dreaming," Jon said, grinning.

Alex narrowed a glance at his brother. "Where's Rachel? She needs to keep her husband in line."

Jon's smile dissolved. He glanced away. "Rachel wasn't able to join me."

Alex shot his brother a disbelieving look. "Rachel isn't coming?"

"Something came up."

"It must have been pretty damned important for her to miss Stephanie's wedding." He persisted, "What's going on, Jon?"

Jon took his time answering. He slammed his sunglasses back into place on the bridge of his nose. "If you must know, she moved out last week."

"Rachel's left you?" Alex asked, the shock hitting him like a blow. "Have you told Mom and Dad?"

"No, and I don't plan to, either." Jon glanced around as though afraid they might be overheard. Satisfied that they were alone, he added, "At least, not until after the wedding. I have no intention of spoiling Stephanie's wedding celebration with my bad news."

Water splashed as Lindsey lifted herself from the side of the pool. She looked like a sea nymph, all wet and sleek and beautiful. Alex swallowed hard, trying to control his body's ill-timed response.

Lindsey smiled a greeting. "Hi, Jon. Glad you finally made it. Your mom's been worried."

"So I've heard," Jon said, returning her smile. Alex fumed silently. His brother wasn't fooling anyone. Behind those mirrored sunglasses of his, he knew that Jon was subjecting Lindsey to a full-body scan. "I'm glad Alex convinced you to join us, Lindsey. The wedding's going to be a lot more fun with you here."

Lindsey sent him an innocent gaze. "It's getting late, Alex. I thought I might go inside to shower and change. I'd also like to give Jamie a call."

Alex nodded. "That's fine. I'll be going in a minute."

Lindsey picked up her towel and left.

Alex told himself he shouldn't be noticing the length of her long legs. But he did. He told himself he shouldn't be watching the hypnotic sway of her slender hips. But he did. He told himself he shouldn't be lusting after a woman who considered him her friend.

But, dammit, he just couldn't seem to help himself.

Jon chuckled. "She's gone now, brother. You can stop drooling."

Alex rose to his feet, nearly toppling the lounge chair in his haste. He pointed an angry finger at his brother. "For the last time, Lindsey and I are just friends. So keep your innuendos to yourself."

"All right," Jon said calmly. "If you're not interested in Lindsey, then that just means she's available for someone else."

Alex saw red. Without thinking, he rasped out the bitter reminder, "Your wife left you less than a week ago, Jon. Maybe you better get your personal life straightened out before you start making moves on another woman."

Jon flinched, but did not allow himself to be deterred

by Alex's show of ill temper. "If it isn't me, Alex, it'll be someone else."

"What the hell's that supposed to mean?"

"It means, brother, you let Lindsey slip through your fingers the first time around with Danny. Don't be stupid enough to let her get away again."

Alex felt the angry heat drain from his body as quickly as if he'd been doused with a bucket of cold water. The warning couldn't have had a greater impact. Jon believed him to have been carrying a torch for his best friend's wife, now his widow. If he could see through his fragile veneer, surely Lindsey must have guessed the truth.

Which would explain a lot.

Like why she'd suddenly shied away from his touch on the beach this afternoon. And why she couldn't quite meet his eyes whenever they spoke. And why she seemed so anxious to rejoin his family rather than spend time alone with him.

He'd worn his heart on his sleeve, and Lindsey had recognized the emotion. And she wasn't impressed.

She'd been running scared ever since.

"Keep your hands to yourself when you're around Lindsey," Alex said, not bothering to hide the threat in his tone. "She doesn't need another complication in her life."

With that he spun on his heel and stomped off toward the house, feeling the need to put some distance between himself and his brother. Anxious, also, to put some distance between himself and his wounded pride.

Chapter Five

At precisely eight o'clock that evening, a knock sounded on her bedroom door. With her hands shaking and her tummy fluttering, Lindsey answered the call.

Alex stood in front of her, dressed in a navy blazer, charcoal-gray slacks and a crisp white shirt, looking cool, calm, and devastatingly handsome. The muted light of her bedside lamp picked up the pale strands of sunlight weaved into his hair. He wore a wicked smile on his lips.

"Hi," he said.

She forced a smile. "Hi."

His gaze lowered, his eyes traveling the length of her body. Slowly, his smile faded. His mouth formed an *O* of surprise. A disbelieving look crossed his face as he stared at her. Or rather, as he stared at her dress.

Self-consciously, she ran a hand over the flared skirt of her red dress. She had almost decided not to wear it. Sleeveless and silky, it showed off her newly acquired tan while clinging to her every curve. She hadn't worn anything so feminine, so alluring, in years. Not since Danny had died.

Considering Alex's reaction, perhaps she should have stuck with something a little less festive. Something black. Widow's weaves, perhaps?

"What's wrong?" she demanded.

"Wrong?" The question seemed to snap him out of his trance. He cleared his throat. "Nothing. Why?"

"You're staring at me," she blurted out.

Like a schoolboy caught pilfering an apple from the teacher's desk, color tinged his cheeks. He brought a hand to the knot of his tie, loosening it slightly.

"It's the dress, isn't it?" She sighed. "It's too bright. I can change. It'll only take a moment."

"No!" The response came quick and loud, startling her.

She narrowed a shrewd glance. "Are you sure you're okay, Alex?"

"I'm fine. The dress—it just reminded me of something." He shook his head, as though trying to dispel the memory. "You look...great. I wouldn't want you to change a thing."

"If you're sure—"

"I'm positive." Quickly regaining his composure, he gave her another resolve-stealing smile.

Her heart gave a tiny lurch of protest as, this time, she found herself to be the one staring. It was those damn lips, she acknowledged silently. Despite her resolve to keep her relationship with Alex strictly platonic, she'd been fantasizing about them all day long. Odd, she'd never noticed how irresistible they were before. At the moment, it took all of her willpower not to haul him into her arms and sample them.

Lindsey attributed her weakened state to their adjoining bedrooms. For the better part of an hour she'd been forced to listen to Alex moving around in his room, preparing for the evening. The sound of the shower running had provoked a bevy of prurient images. But even the simplest of sounds—the slamming of a drawer, the opening of a closet door and the rustle of clothing being slipped into place—had sent her pulse racing and her body humming with possibilities. It wasn't any wonder that her hormones would be running rampant now.

He offered her his arm. "Shall we go?"

Lindsey bit her strawberry-glossed lips, considering the offer. In her present unpredictable state of mind, getting too close to Alex might not be a good idea. Short of being rude, however, she didn't know how she could refuse. Hesitantly she placed her hand in the crook of his arm. As she had expected, a jolt of awareness rocked her.

Seemingly oblivious to her reaction, he led her down the hall. He shortened his long-legged stride, strolling at a leisurely pace. Arm in arm, hip brushing against hip, his spicy aftershave enveloping her like a cloud, Lindsey felt as though she were going into sensory overload. She gave a silent moan of frustration. It truly was going to be a long, long evening.

"Lindsey?"

She blinked and peered up into a pair of concerned blue eyes.

"Are you sure you're all right?" he asked.

"I'm fine. Why?"

"I asked about your call to Jamie, only you didn't answer. There's nothing wrong, is there? If there is, we can catch the next flight—"

"Jamie's fine," she said, feeling a flush of embarrassment warm her cheeks. "In fact, he couldn't be better. He's having a great time. He watched the parades on TV this morning, then stuffed himself with turkey and pumpkin pie this afternoon. He said to tell you hello for him and, if it wasn't too much trouble, would you please bring him back some seashells for his nature collection.''

Alex's smile returned. "That's my boy."

The words nearly stopped her. Her step faltered. Quickly, she struggled to regain her poise. In a heartbeat, Lindsey realized exactly what had been bothering her these past few months. Alex was becoming more than just a positive male influence in Jamie's life; she'd allowed him to become a father figure.

But Alex wasn't Jamie's father.

Danny was.

No matter how tempting the support might be, she couldn't expect Alex to take Danny's place.

"I think I've lost you again," Alex said, his deep voice vibrating in her ears.

Lindsey forced a smile. "I'm sorry. I don't know what's wrong with me tonight. My mind's a million miles away."

"Maybe not a million. More like a few hundred." He quirked a questioning brow. "Say, as far as St. Louis and Jamie?"

"You know me too well," she said, keeping her tone light.

His expression sobered. Without a trace of humor, he said, "Funny, I would have said I don't know you nearly well enough."

The statement shocked her, taking her unaware. Before she had time to respond, however, they stepped into the dining room where Alex's family awaited them.

Seven pairs of eyes swept across the room, riveting them with frankly curious gazes.

Lindsey stopped dead in her tracks. If it weren't for Alex holding on tightly to her arm, she'd have turned on her heel and run from the room. She'd never felt so intimidated before in her life.

"Lindsey, I hope you're hungry. We have enough food to feed an army," Mrs. Trent said, the first to greet her.

"Sorry I missed you this afternoon, m'dear," Alex's father, a tall, distinguished-looking man with dark, silvering hair, added. He mimicked a golf swing. "I had a meeting that couldn't be canceled."

Their friendly banter worked to soothe her nervous misgivings. She felt the tension ease from her muscles.

Jon, Alex's brother, handed her a glass of wine. "You look beautiful, tonight, Lindsey."

Alex pulled her closer, tightening the protective grip of his arm.

Stephanie joined them, trailing a slender, dark-haired and extremely handsome man behind her. "Lindsey, Alex, you haven't met my fiancé, Jeffrey Dolan. Jeffrey, this is my brother Alex and his—" There was only the slightest hesitation, as though she were searching for the appropriate description, before adding, "His friend, Lindsey."

Reluctantly, Alex released the possessive grip he'd held on her arm and extended a hand to greet his future brother-in-law. Lindsey felt an instant chill, missing the warmth and security of his body next to hers.

The handshake was noticeably brief.

"Lindsey, it's a pleasure," Jeffrey said, turning to her. He flashed her an appreciative glance, leaving no part of her anatomy untouched. His handshake was limp and weak, lingering a bit longer than necessary.

Discomfitted, Lindsey was first to break the contact.

"Now that everyone's here, let's eat," Mr. Trent announced.

Mrs. Trent led the way to the long marble-and-glass table. The table was set with fine bone china, ornate silver, and sparkling crystal glassware. A cornucopia with fresh flowers, miniature pumpkins and squash, flanked by tall, tapering candles, served as the centerpiece. The effect was elegant yet cozy.

"Lindsey, you sit here." Alex's mother patted the back of a chair. She pointed to a spot on the opposite side of the table. "Alex, you're over there."

Alex started to protest.

His mother waved away his objections. "Now, I don't want to hear a word. You can have Lindsey all to yourself in St. Louis. The rest of us would like a chance to get to know her."

Moments later, Lindsey found herself sitting between Jon and Jeffrey. She glanced across the table at Alex, who looked none too pleased with the situation. Their gazes met and held. Then, with a shrug and a shake of his head, Alex gave in to a smile. A smile Lindsey couldn't help but return. Long forgotten, an unmistakable warmth blossomed throughout her body. Awareness, pure and simple.

The turkey was brought in, prompting the obligatory oohs and aahs. Lindsey was glad for the diversion, sure that in another moment Alex would see the lust in her eyes.

"Exactly what do you do in St. Louis, Lindsey?" Jeffrey asked, his voice unexpectedly close.

Lindsey whipped around to find Stephanie's fiancé

leaning toward her. She flashed him a nervous smile, composing her jangled nerves. "I'm a mother and a teacher, Mr. Dolan."

"Jeffrey, please." He inched his way nearer. So close, she could smell the minty freshness of his breath. In a tone meant for her ears only, he added, "It's a pity you don't live closer. We have such a short time to get to know each other."

The words may have sounded proper enough, but the glint in his eye was anything but innocent. The groom-to-be had lech written all over him. As a matter of self-protection, Lindsey scooted her chair a tad closer to Jon's.

Jeffrey had the nerve to look pleased by her skittishness.

In her haste to escape Jeffrey's obnoxious presence, her elbow connected with Jon's, interrupting his conversation with his father. He gave her a polite smile, turning his attention to her. Gratefully, Lindsey sought refuge in Jon's company.

After a bumpy start, the meal progressed smoothly. The friendly conversation of a close-knit family filled the air. Lindsey listened with an envious ear to the tales of Thanksgivings past.

Stephanie regaled them with the story of the Thanksgiving when an idealistic, eleven-year-old Alex donated their turkey to the local food pantry. Their mother added that that was the year they'd had Chinese carry-out to accompany the cranberries and mashed potatoes.

Alex retaliated with a memory of Thanksgiving during Stephanie's senior year in high school when she—along with everyone else in the family—had suffered through a breakup with her high school sweetheart.

Lindsey smiled at the exchange. Her own memories

of Thanksgiving weren't nearly as pleasant. When she
was five, her mother had been very ill during Thanksgiving. By Christmas she had died, losing her battle with
cancer. From then on, despite her father's efforts to the
contrary, the holidays had been somber occasions.

Dessert chased away the bittersweet memories. In ad-
dition to the traditional pumpkin pie, they were given a
choice of chocolate mousse or fruit tarts. Lindsey chose
the chocolate, of course. She scooped a spoonful of the
rich mousse into her mouth. Just as it slid luxuriously
down her throat, the unexpected happened.

A stocking-covered foot snaked its way under the table until it rested neatly on top of hers.

Lindsey nearly choked on her dessert. She gave a tiny
yelp of surprise, her eyes flying to Alex's. Alex? Impossible. Given the direction of the assault and the ample
foot space under the table, there could be no mistake.
Jeffrey was the one playing footsie under the table.

Her cheeks burned with embarrassment as all eyes,
including those of Alex, focused upon her. Not wanting
to cause a scene, she mumbled a quick apology for her
outburst.

Unfortunately, the attention did not deter her auda-
cious interloper. In fact, Jeffrey grew even bolder. Lindsey froze as his foot slid upward, past her ankle, her
shin... The man must be a contortionist, she decided.

Appalled, Lindsey shifted in her chair, crossing her
legs and surreptitiously ending the besiegement.

The move brought her even closer to Jon.

A frown flitted across Alex's brow.

Jon smiled down at her, his gaze curious.

Lindsey wished the ground would open up and swallow her whole, saving her from this awkward situation.
She'd never been more embarrassed in her life.

Obviously not one to take a hint, Jeffrey continued his under-the-table manuevers. At the next brush of his stocking-covered foot, Lindsey dropped her spoon and nearly jumped onto Jon's lap.

Curious glances were exchanged around the table.

Alex's frown grew into a scowl. From the look in his eyes, he appeared primed to throttle someone. Her? Or his brother? Or, perhaps, both of them? She wasn't sure.

"Are you all right, Lindsey?" Jon asked, his gaze now concerned.

"Fine, fine," she muttered, detangling herself from Jon's arms. Determinedly, she retrieved her spoon. "Just caught a chill, that's all."

"Perhaps it's the mousse, m'dear," Mr. Trent suggested helpfully.

Lindsey gave a weak smile.

The foot returned.

This time she was ready for the attack. Anger spurring her into action, Lindsey spiked her three-inch heel into the fleshy part of Jeffrey's arch.

Jeffrey flinched, but did not yell out.

Lindsey allowed herself a moment of triumph as she watched him stand and excuse himself. She felt no remorse when he limped out of the dining room, heading straight for the powder room.

Her victory was short-lived, however, when she felt the heavy weight of someone watching her. An unsmiling Alex was staring at her. If the look in his eyes was any indication, he was not amused by her dining room decorum.

Coffee was served in the living room in front of a roaring fire. The family was seated comfortably throughout the room. Jeffrey stood next to Stephanie's chair, noticeably favoring one foot over the other. Alex's father stood at the fireplace; his mother held court on the settee.

Alex shared the sofa with Lindsey and Jon. He wasn't exactly sure what had transpired during dinner, but he was taking no chances. Eyeing his brother warily, he kept a possessive arm draped lightly across Lindsey's shoulder. A decision that proved to be sweet torture.

For over an hour, while half listening to his family's discussion of the wedding plans, he'd been struggling with a faltering self-control. It was the dress, he told himself. The same red dress Lindsey had worn in his erotic dream. All silky and sexy, his eyes had nearly popped out when he'd first spotted her wearing the damn thing.

She'd looked better than any fantasy.

Alex loosened the knot of his tie, blaming the heat of the fireplace for the liquid warmth coursing through him. If he even considered the real reason, he'd be a goner.

Lindsey chose that moment to shift in her seat, flexing her neck slightly. Then with a yawn, she melted against him. Her slender curves fit neatly into the niche of his body. The smooth skin of her bare shoulders grazed his fingertips. Her delicate perfume wafted up to tease his nostrils.

Alex froze. He felt as though he'd been hit with a cannon ball of white heat aimed directly at areas south of the border. How was he supposed to get through the rest of the evening pretending to be a gentleman with Lindsey plastered against him? This evening? Hell, he had the rest of the weekend to worry about.

Lindsey's actions didn't go unnoticed by the rest of the family, either.

"Where are our manners?" Alex's mother declared.

"It's late, and we're keeping our guest up. Alex, why don't you see Lindsey to her room?"

It wasn't really that late, not even eleven o'clock. But Alex didn't argue. Considering his tenuous grip on self-control, he was more than ready for the evening to end.

Alex stood, reaching a hand to help her to her feet. Lindsey didn't think twice but to accept. Goodbyes were exchanged. They were ushered out of the room on a cloud of goodwill.

Which lasted all of about thirty seconds. Once out of the earshot of his family, Alex reacted to his hormonal upheaval in a typical male fashion. He blamed Lindsey.

Glaring at her, he demanded, "You want to tell me what's going on between you and Jon?"

"Me and Jon?" she repeated, looking confused.

"You heard me," he growled, unable to stop the out-of-control freight train of jealousy that sped through him. He quickened his pace, his long legs eating up the carpeted hallway.

With her hand still firmly held in his, Lindsey hurried to keep up with him. "Alex, you're being ridiculous."

"Ridiculous?" he growled. "I'm not blind, Lindsey. Something was definitely happening during dinner."

"Oh, that," Lindsey sighed. "Alex, you'll never believe this but—"

"I realize you haven't had much experience with men lately," he cut in, unable to keep the anger from his tone. "But surely you must know what kind of signals you were throwing out there tonight."

She sucked in a shocked breath. "Signals?"

"Lindsey, I brought you here so that you'd have a chance to rest and recuperate," he broke in again. He stormed up the stairs, taking her along for the ride. With a sharp turn toward their bedrooms, he continued, "Not to satisfy any latent urgings."

Lindsey, it would seem, had had enough. She yanked her hand from his. "Is that what you really think happened here tonight? That I was making a play for Jon?"

Her anger didn't really surprise him. He'd been acting like a jealous fool. She had every right to be peeved.

"A married man?" Her voice shook with emotion. "Do you really think I'd have so little respect for the marriage vow to even consider such a thing?"

The question struck him like a blow. He felt as though he'd been slapped in the face with the bitter truth. In his self-righteous tirade of jealousy, he'd forgotten one thing. He was guilty of the very misdeed of which he'd accused her.

While she was married to his best friend, with his heart and body, he'd lusted after Lindsey.

At his continued silence, Lindsey growled her frustration. Tears of anger—or perhaps, disappointment—filled her eyes. "I thought you knew me better than that, Alex. How could you think so low of me?"

Before he could react, she spun on her heel and strode the short distance to her bedroom. The slamming of the door behind her reverberated throughout the hall. Alex winced at the noise, but did not move. He felt rooted to the spot.

He didn't know if he had the strength to go on. His own stupidity may have cost him more than a friendship. It may have cost him any chance he'd had with the only woman he would ever love.

He may have lost Lindsey for good.

Coming to Florida with Alex had been a mistake. First thing tomorrow morning, she would have to leave.

Two hours later, Lindsey sat in her bed, her knees tucked beneath her chin, uneasily considering her decision. Their argument had ruined the entire weekend. Staying would surely put a damper on the wedding festivities. It seemed the most logical course of action to put distance between her and Alex.

So why did it feel as though she would be running away? That, if she left, she'd be causing even more damage to their relationship?

She gave a bitter laugh. What relationship?

After tonight, she sincerely doubted if she and Alex could continue being friends. Her chest ached with the loss. His anger had been uncalled for. His accusation, unjust. Didn't he realize, she, of all people, would be the last to consider an extramarital affair?

The very thought repulsed her, dredging up too many bitter memories. She fought to keep them at bay.

Alex's behavior had been so unlike him. He'd ranted and raved like a...like a jealous suitor.

Alex, jealous? She frowned. Impossible.

Her frown deepened. Or was it?

She'd be the first to admit things hadn't been the same between them since their plane left St. Louis. They'd been on pins and needles, struggling to find the right way to act around each other. She'd blamed herself for the discomfort. It had been years since she'd been alone with a man, other than her brother. She didn't know how to behave.

But perhaps she wasn't the only one whose feelings had changed.

Lindsey laid back in her bed, pulling the bedcovers over her face, frustrated by the circles her mind seemed to be spinning in. The worse part of the situation was that the one person whom she could always turn to when she was feeling confused, the one person who always seemed ready to listen to any of her problems—no matter how trivial they might be—was Alex.

Tonight she'd lost more than a confidant. She'd lost her best friend.

A knock sounded softly on the patio door.

Lindsey tensed, debating whether to answer. Chances were good that the late-night caller was Alex. But what if it was Stephanie's lecherous fiancé, Jeffrey? No matter which, she'd rather not deal with either of the two men.

"Lindsey," a deep, male voice whispered.

Relief worked its way through her body as she recognized the voice. It was Alex.

As quickly as it had formed, her relief disappeared. Anger fought to regain a foothold. She was, after all, supposed to be mad at Alex, she reminded herself.

"I know you're awake," he persisted. "I can see your light on through the curtains."

"Go away, Alex," she said. "I'm tired. I don't want to talk to you."

Silence stretched for an eternity.

Half-disappointed that he'd given up so easily, Lindsey had almost decided he'd left when suddenly the door opened and Alex barged into the room.

The nerve of the man!

She sat up in bed. Like a flustered Victorian virgin, she stammered, "Get—get out of my bedroom!"

The covers slipped to her waist, revealing a healthy amount of pajama-unclad flesh. Her state of near undress didn't go unnoticed by Alex. Like lightning to a rod, his blue-eyed gaze zeroed in on her bare shoulders and silky white negligee.

Scowling, Lindsey pulled the covers up around her

neck. "Go away, Alex. I think we've both said enough for one evening—"

"You're right," he said, surprising her by agreeing. "We've said too much. That's the problem."

He paused, drawing a hand through his thick curls of blond hair, his frustration obvious. For the first time she noticed the tension lining his face. Since the last time she'd seen him, he'd lost his jacket and tie. With his shirt unbuttoned and his shirtcuffs rolled up to reveal strong forearms, he looked disheveled and dangerous.

Lindsey shivered with trepidation.

Oblivious to her reaction, Alex paced the floor between her bed and the patio doors. He ran his fingers through his hair, again. A gesture he'd obviously repeated often in the last few hours. She'd never seen Alex look quite so distraught.

He stopped pacing long enough to fix a determined look on her face. "Lindsey, I've come to apologize."

He stepped closer to her bed.

Lindsey cowered beneath the bedcovers. Get a grip, she chastised herself, the patio doors were wide open. If he'd come to ravish her, surely he'd have closed the doors after himself. The thought left her dealing with an uneasy sense of disappointment.

"I said some things that were totally out of line." He gave his head a miserable shake. "I don't know what came over me."

She knew.

They were in a romantic paradise, alone for the first time in their lives without Rick or Jamie to act as their chaperones. Their nice safe routine was gone. It wasn't any wonder that they didn't know how to behave around each other.

Lindsey gulped in a deep breath of air as he sat next to her on the edge of her bed.

Less than an arm's length from touching, he studied her with an unwavering intensity. "We've known each other for a long time. You're one of my best friends, Lindsey. I don't want to lose you."

She found her voice, trembling though it was. "I don't want to lose you, either."

He relaxed visibly. A tentative smile eased across his face. "Still friends?"

She nodded.

He sighed his relief. "Thank goodness."

Then, before she knew what was happening, he enveloped her in a hug. A tender, innocent embrace.

Her reaction was anything but innocent. Her breath caught. Her pulse quickened. Liquid heat spilled throughout her veins.

Alex was putting her through hormonal hell.

He pulled away, but didn't release her.

She stared at him, wide-eyed and uncertain. For a moment she was afraid he might kiss her. Afraid he wouldn't.

He did. Kiss her, that is.

Right on the middle of her forehead. A nice, platonic kiss. The kind she'd seen him give Jamie a hundred times, when telling him goodbye.

Her disappointment must have been obvious. His gaze lingered on her face. He frowned slightly. "You're sure everything's all right now?"

"Of course." She forced a smile. "I don't hold grudges, Alex."

She'd had enough practice forgiving and forgetting with Danny. He had disappointed her often in the past. Why should Alex be any different?

"Well, it's been a long day." Yet he didn't move to leave. He hesitated, looking as though he wanted to say more.

"Was there anything else?" she prompted him.

"About dinner," he began. "What happened with Jon...do you want to talk about it?"

This was her chance to explain, to tell him about that stinker of a future brother-in-law he was getting. But something stopped her.

Trust stopped her.

If Alex had believed her capable of flirting with his own brother, what would stop him from thinking she'd deliberately encouraged the advances of his sister's fiancé? It was a matter of trust. And to be honest, she wasn't sure if she trusted Alex enough to not react badly if she told him the truth.

Once burned, twice as cautious.

After the disillusionment of her marriage to Danny, she wondered if she'd ever be able to completely trust another man. Slowly, she shook her head. "I'd rather not discuss it right now, Alex."

He sighed. "Maybe later."

"Perhaps," she said carefully.

He rose then, pulling himself to his full six-foot-two-inch height. He smiled, a quick, troubled smile. "Well, then...good night, Lindsey."

"Good night, Alex."

He left the same way he'd entered, through the patio doors. This time, he made certain they were closed behind him. The click of the doors being shut echoed in her ears.

Lindsey stared at the door, envisioning the man who'd just left, wondering why it felt as though he'd closed the door on their future, as well.

Chapter Six

The next morning Lindsey awoke with sore muscles from yesterday's swim and a throbbing headache from lack of sleep. A night of tossing and turning had left her groggy, sapped of her usual energy. Her dreams, when she'd been able to sleep, had been unsettling.

She'd dreamed of Danny.

At first she'd blamed herself for his death. They had argued the last time she had seen him. After months of suspicion, he had finally admitted the truth. He'd had an extramarital affair. He'd wanted her forgiveness. She'd been unable to comply. She would never forget the look on Danny's face when she told him she didn't know if she could go on…that their marriage may be beyond repair.

He'd left her then, angry and upset.

And he'd never come back.

It wasn't until early the next morning, when Rick had arrived on her doorstep, that she knew Danny was dead. Friends on the force who knew the family thought it best she heard the news from her brother, not from one of the uniform blues. For that much she was grateful. But that didn't stop the pain, the unspeakable guilt from forming.

Even after she'd been assured the accident hadn't been Danny's fault, she still blamed herself. If he hadn't been upset, perhaps he'd have reacted quicker to the drunk driver who'd veered into his lane of traffic. If she had given him the absolution he'd sought, perhaps Danny would never have left in the first place.

Since then, Danny had haunted her dreams often. Over and over she had relived their final and fateful argument, wishing she could take back every angry word she'd said.

Last night, her dream had been different.

Danny had been different. More like his old self, the impulsive charmer who'd caught her eye before he'd been burdened with the responsibility of a wife and child. Finally, he'd seemed at peace.

Lindsey threw back the covers, pushing the dream from her mind. It was early, the sun barely rising. But she needed to get up, get out, clear her head of cluttered thoughts.

She dressed quickly in a T-shirt, shorts and tennis shoes. Grabbing a light jacket, she hurried from her room, using the patio door as her escape route.

The air, sprinkled with a tangy scent of salt water, bathed her skin. She breathed deeply, shivering as a cool breeze stroked her bare limbs. Pulling on her jacket, she strode toward the beach.

Her feet sank into the sand, the grit working its way into her tennis shoes. Shucking them off, she edged her way closer to the lapping waves of water. It felt shockingly cold, turning her feet pink and tingly.

She quickened her pace, hurrying to get nowhere fast, not allowing herself the chance to wonder at what, or from whom, she was escaping. Focusing her eyes straight ahead on the seemingly endless strip of beach, she closed her mind to the world around her. Without a backward glance, she began running, leaving the house and her troubled thoughts far behind.

Until, her lungs burning and her heart pounding, she stumbled to a stop. She dragged in a labored breath as her legs collapsed beneath her weight. The sand cushioned her fall as she landed on the beach and stared at the crashing waves of water.

Slowly, her surroundings seeped into her consciousness. Somewhere nearby a woman's voice called a good-bye. A car door slammed and the motor revved to life. Hand in hand, an older couple walked along the shoreline. Seagulls fought the morning tide for their breakfast, scampering back and forth, dodging the frothy waves of water.

A world of activity surrounded her. She was only a mile, maybe more, from the Trents's home. Yet she'd never felt so alone...so adrift, in all her life.

Somehow, she'd lost her way. Certain whichever direction she chose, it would be the wrong one. Drawing up her legs, circling her arms about her knees, she curled up into a tight knot of confusion.

Her confusion was from within, she realized. She knew exactly where she was in a physical sense. It was her heart that didn't know which path to take.

In her dream of Danny at peace, he seemed to be giving her his approval, telling her it was time to forget the past and to get on with her future. Her undeniable disappointment at Alex's innocent kiss revealed she needed more, so much more than living a solitary existence. But fear knotted her stomach every time she considered…the more.

These past two years had been filled with changes. She'd endured the loss of a husband for whom, though their marriage may have been troubled, she had cared deeply. She'd survived financial chaos, turning a desperate situation into one that was strained but manageable. She'd handled the burden of raising a child on her own, taking pride in the wonderful young man Jamie was becoming.

But what she hadn't been able to change were the long, empty nights.

Loneliness ached in her heart, throbbing like an unattended wound, keeping her awake into the wee hours of the morning. It was only when the sun rose, when her days were too busy and hectic to allow her the time to dwell on her own needs, that she found refuge.

But now, even her sanctum of daylight had turned on her. The bright rays of sunshine could not hide that which was lacking in her life. She needed a companion, a soulmate…she needed someone to love.

The wind whipped her hair into her eyes. She raised a hand to brush the lock from her face. Her wedding ring shimmered dully in the sunlight. Lindsey stared at the gold band, her heart thumping against her chest.

After two years she'd never found the courage to take off the ring. It served as a constant reminder of the uncertainty with which her marriage to Danny ended, of the unfinished business that remained between her and Danny. At one time, ridding herself of the ring felt as though she were ridding herself of his memory.

Now she wondered if keeping the ring really meant she'd found an excuse not to get on with her life, of seeking the companionship she craved.

An image of Alex's handsome face cropped up in her mind. Last night she'd wanted more from him than a fleeting kiss. She had wanted to taste the sweet heat of his lips. She'd wanted to feel the warmth of his body covering hers. She'd wanted to feel alive beneath his touch.

She had wanted…Alex.

Lindsey stood, abruptly whisking the sand from her legs and the unsettling thoughts from her mind. Then, before she lost her courage, she twisted her wedding ring from her finger. A weight felt as though it had been lifted from her hand, and from her heart. Silently, she tucked the gold band into the pocket of her shorts, knowing she'd taken the first step in saying goodbye to Danny, and the first step in getting on with her life.

What part Alex would play in her life remained to be seen. If last night's brotherly peck on the forehead was any indication, an intimate relationship seemed doubtful. She should be glad they had settled their differences, that they still had their friendship.

Only she didn't feel glad.

She felt restless.

She headed back to the house, and to Alex, at a slower pace. She dug her toes into the cold, wet sand. She lifted her face and let the sun and the salty breeze off the water caress her skin. The beautiful morning worked its magic. She'd almost forgotten her troubles when the unwanted occurred.

Jeffrey, Stephanie's obnoxious fiancé, stood on the beach, blocking her path to the house.

"Good morning, Lindsey," he drawled, his voice as slippery as oiled skin. His bare feet and Ray·Ban sunglasses were an incongruous match to his dress slacks and tailored shirt. Rumpled, and sporting a morning beard, he looked as though he'd just tumbled out of someone's bed.

"A little early for a visit, isn't it, Mr. Dolan?" she asked, not bothering with social niceties.

His perfect white teeth glinted as he smiled. "It was late before the evening wound down. Mrs. Trent insisted I stay the night...in a guest room, of course." The derision in his tone was unmistakable. Obviously, he hadn't been pleased with the sleeping accommodations. "Just a couple of doors down from yours, actually. I heard you leave this morning. I've been waiting for you to return."

The thought of him being so close sent shivers down her spine. Without thinking, she quipped, "Thank goodness I had the forethought to lock my door last night."

He studied her, an amused glint in his eye. "You don't like me."

"After last night? Not really," she admitted.

"I could change that—" he stepped closer, his presence overpowering, intimidating "—if you'd give me the chance."

Despite the butterflies dancing in her stomach, she held her ground. "Mr. Dolan, the only chance I'm going to give you is to back up and get out of my way. My father was a police officer. I know how to protect myself from perverts."

He held up his hands in mock surrender, but didn't move. "There's no need for threats. If you want to go, then go. It's your loss."

Disgusted, Lindsey shook her head. "You're supposed to be getting married tomorrow. Don't you think you should be concentrating on your wedding vows?"

He chuckled. "I've always favored an open approach to marriage."

"Does Stephanie know about your approaches?"

His smile tightened. "Stephanie's always been willing to take an enlightened view of life."

Lindsey stared at him, incredulous. Was there any man left in the world who took a commitment seriously? Or were those who believed in the words love, honor and cherish a dying breed?

"In other words, what you don't tell her, won't hurt *you*," she said. "Maybe it's time someone else let her know just what kind of man you really are."

He shrugged. "It'll be their word against mine."

"You really are a jerk, aren't you?"

"No need to be upset, Lindsey," he cooed silkily, tsk-tsking as he angled closer. "You really ought to learn to relax, enjoy life more."

Lindsey watched his approach warily and considered her options. Fight? Or flight? Last night she'd been armed with a pair of three-inch spike heels. Today she was barefoot and ill-equipped to handle any unwanted advances. Jeffrey might be a slimeball, but he was over six foot and in good shape. If it came to a battle of wills, she'd lose hands-down.

Which left only one choice: flight.

Not giving herself time to reconsider, Lindsey side-stepped Jeffrey's roadblock and sprinted toward the house. Her heart pounding, she didn't look back to see if she was being followed. She kept her eyes straight ahead, trained on the bank of patio doors on the wide, stone veranda, desperately trying to remember which one was hers.

Alex stepped out of the shower and flicked a towel off the rack. The icy water had done little to cool his overheated libido. He scowled, feeling grumpy and out of sorts. In his waking hours, he may be celibate and a model of wholesomeness, but in his dreams, he was as naughty as he wanted to be. And to be honest, his lustful escapades were wearing him out.

Lindsey, of course, had a recurring role in his nightly fantasies.

Last night, seeing her in that big, comfy bed, dressed in a flimsy negligee, looking sweet and all so sexy, had set off a firestorm of prurient notions. Holding her in his arms had been sheer torture. He'd been a heartbeat away from fulfilling his fantasies when he'd seen the confused, almost-terrified look in her eyes. It had taken all of his strength not to give in to his wants and make sweet love to her.

Alex moaned and pushed the thought from his mind. He wrapped the towel around his waist and stepped into his bedroom. His willpower was at an all-time low. He didn't know how much more temptation he could take before his self-control snapped.

He reached for the drawer for his briefs, and the patio door sprang open.

Lindsey slammed into the room, shutting the door behind her with a thud. Slowly, she turned to face him. Taking one look at him, she froze. Her face flushed, her dark hair tangled about her shoulders, breathless and excited, she looked like a dream come true. She looked like *his* dream come true.

His heart jackhammered in his chest. Liquid heat pulsed through his blood. Alex swallowed hard and willed his unpredictable body to behave.

"Alex?" she asked, looking confused.

In what he hoped was a casual stance, he leaned an arm against the dresser, and quirked an eyebrow in question. "Were you expecting someone else?"

"Yes...I mean no." She blushed. Like a butterfly, her gaze flitted over him before moving away. "I thought this room was mine, not yours."

"Aha," he said, waiting for her to make the next move. Considering his current state of mind and dress, a quick exit would be advisable.

She seemed in no hurry to leave, however. Biting her lip, she parted the curtains and glanced anxiously out the closed patio door. "So what do you think about your future brother-in-law?"

"Jeffrey?" The question surprised him, taking him aback. "He's all right, I guess. Not exactly the kind of guy I pictured Stephanie marrying, though."

Lindsey looked at him, her eyes wide and wondering. Just as quickly, she averted her gaze. "Oh? Why do you say that?"

Lindsey, it would appear, wanted to strike up a conversation.

Alex gave a silent moan of frustration. Now he knew what hell was like. He was experiencing it firsthand. It was having something he desperately wanted dangled before his eyes, but being denied the opportunity to indulge.

He shrugged, trying his best not to appear disconcerted. "Stephanie's always been a real go-getter. She's smart, savvy, and has the determination of a bulldozer. Jeffrey seems a little too laid-back to keep up with her."

"Yeah," Lindsey said, nodding. She took a deep breath, her breasts straining against the thin fabric of her T-shirt. "I know what you mean."

Heat flushed his skin. His mouth went dry. Alex licked his parched lips and tried not to stare at the more enticing parts of her anatomy. He failed miserably.

She lifted a corner of the curtain, again, and peered outside. "So what are our plans for the day?"

"Errands," he said, wincing as his voice cracked. "My mother's got a whole list of jobs for us to do before the wedding."

"Hmm…" Then she proceeded to chat, telling him something about her early morning walk, apparently in no hurry to leave.

He listened for all of about five seconds. Unable to help himself, he studied her long, slender legs, the curve of her hips, the gentle swell of her breasts, and sighed. Life was not fair. He'd spent a restless night trying to get the image of Lindsey in her bed, in her pajamas, out of his mind. Now, first thing in the morning, she's there, bringing with her a new flood of lustful longing pulsing through his loins.

The trouble was, Alex decided, shifting uncomfortably, he was just in too vulnerable of a position. Now if they were both naked, that would be a different story. But since he was the only one undressed, keeping his feelings for Lindsey underwrap, so to speak, was proving to be a difficult task.

Alex had a growing problem, literally.

Dead silence filled the room.

He felt the prickling sensation of Lindsey watching him. His gaze flew to her face. "Something wrong?"

"You aren't listening, are you?" she asked, her tone accusatory.

Irritation flashed, his patience snapped. "Believe me, Lindsey. I have a much longer attention span when I'm fully dressed."

As though seeing him for the first time, Lindsey looked at him…at all of him. Her face flushed a deep crimson. Obviously flustered, she started backing up,

making her way toward the door. Her foot caught on the
rug, nearly tripping her.

"I'll...um, see you—er—talk to you later, Alex."

He sighed. "G'bye, Lindsey."

She left as she had entered, in a whirlwind of feminine
discomposure, the door slamming behind her as she disappeared from sight.

Alex sank onto the bed and cursed fate, the stars, and
any other force that might be working against him. Well,
hell, he told himself, he'd really let the cat out of the
bag this time. He meant that in a figurative sense, of
course, as well as a physical one.

If there'd been any doubts in Lindsey's mind before,
they were gone now. She certainly knew of his attraction
to her. Some things were a little hard—an understate-
ment, for sure—to hide.

An unexpected relief rushed through him. He'd been
pretending to be just her friend for so damn long, he
hadn't realized how good it would feel for the truth to
be out in the open. Of course, he'd have rather have told
her in his own words. But, then again, some actions
painted a much clearer picture.

He rolled his eyes. It didn't matter how she'd found
out his feelings for her. The important thing was that she
knew.

The question now was, what should he do about it?
Should he go to her and try to explain? Or pretend that
nothing had happened and hope for the best?

Neither solution settled well in his stomach.

It was too late to explain or to try to ignore the matter.
The truth was out there. He'd done his part in changing
their relationship. The next step was up to Lindsey.

Alex's mother, bless her heart, unwittingly gave Lindsey time to compose her jangled nerves before having

to be alone with Alex again.

Earlier, over breakfast at the huge oak table in the kitchen, Alex's mother had said firmly, "Now, I don't want to hear any arguments. The plans are already made. Alex, you and Jon will help me with my errands. Lindsey, you'll keep Stephanie busy by accompanying her to the Pink Flamingo, one of Whisper Key's finest, full-service salons. She's been on pins and needles all week. Someone has to make sure she doesn't get nervous today. And, frankly, I just don't have the time."

Wordlessly, Alex had reached for the sugar bowl. His arm brushed hers, sending shock waves of electricity up her limb. Warily, he stole a sideways glance at her.

And Lindsey's heart had thudded in her chest. Since leaving his bedroom that morning, she'd been in a state of tension. Seeing Alex almost naked in a skimpy towel had been enough to set her hormones in a frenzy. Seeing Alex in a full state of arousal had set her mind racing with myriad confusing emotions.

First on the list was a purely feminine sense of pride. She'd reveled in the knowledge that he wasn't as immune to her as she had believed. Trepidation followed closely on the heels of pride. There was no turning back; their relationship had been irrevocably changed. Sex had a way of screwing up the best of friendships. And last, but not least, she'd felt anticipation. What, exactly, would happen next?

What had happened next was that Alex gave her a hesitant smile and a shrug of resignation as he spooned sugar onto his grapefruit. Lindsey couldn't believe it. The rat was acting as though nothing earthshaking had happened between them! If she didn't know better, she'd have said he almost looked relieved that they wouldn't be spending the day alone.

Several hours later, with her hair wrapped in a towel, a herbal masque drying on her face and cotton balls stuck between her toes to prevent her pedicured toenails from smudging, Lindsey determinedly pushed all thoughts of Alex aside and concentrated on the task at hand.

"Good grief, I feel so lazy," she moaned. "You're going to have to roll me off this chair just to get me home."

Stephanie lifted a cucumber slice from her eye and squinted at her. "If you think this is good, wait until Elsa gives you a full body massage. Your muscles will feel like putty in her hands."

Lindsey sighed. "It was wonderful of your mother to treat us to a day of pampering. I can't remember the last time I felt so relaxed."

"Then her plan worked." Stephanie grinned at Lindsey's shocked expression. "You didn't really believe her story about my prewedding jitters, did you? Mom's been fretting over you like a baby chick since the moment you arrived. She took one look at you and decided to take you under her wing."

Lindsey winced. "I'll admit I've been a little tired lately. But, surely, I didn't look that bad, did I?"

"The truth? You looked so beat, I'd have thought a strong wind could have knocked you for a loop." Stephanie's smile faded. "Losing Danny must have been awful. Alex told us these last couple of years haven't been easy for you."

"Alex worries too much," Lindsey said, shifting uncomfortably beneath the concern. "I'm fine, really."

"I'm sure you are," Stephanie assured her quickly.

"It's just being alone with a child to raise—it must be difficult."

"I'm not alone. I have my brother…and Alex." She hesitated, feeling the need to explain. "Alex has been a big help with Jamie. He's gone out of his way to care about his godson."

"And his godson's mother," Stephanie added, chuckling. "I've never seen my big brother so smitten before."

Lindsey's cheeks itched beneath the masque as her face warmed with embarrassment. "Stephanie, Alex and I…we aren't really involved. He sees other women. And I…well, I just haven't felt up to dating anyone yet."

Stephanie snorted her disbelief. "Just how often do you see Alex?"

Lindsey shrugged. "I don't know. A couple of times a week. Maybe more. But it's not what you think. Jamie's the reason—"

"I know my brother, Lindsey. He's got a heart of gold, but he isn't a saint. For that much loyalty, he has to have more of an incentive than being a doting godfather. Besides, I've seen the way he looks at you."

"Looks at me?"

"Like you're a gooey dessert that he'd like to eat up whole." Stephanie laughed. "Come on, Lindsey. Surely you've noticed."

"No…well, m-maybe," she stammered as images of Alex in a bath towel flashed through her mind. She closed her eyes and dropped her head against the cushioned headrest. "This is the darnedest conversation I've ever had. Alex is sweet and supportive, and one of the most attractive men I've ever met. But he's still Alex. His track record speaks for itself. He isn't ready to settle down, any more than I'm ready for a fling."

"You're wrong, Lindsey. Alex is the most dependable man I've ever known. When the right woman comes along, he'll be ready for the Big C. Commitment." She wagged the engagement ring on her left hand. "I'd bet my diamond on that."

Stephanie's engagement ring brought an unwanted image of Jeffrey skittering through her mind. In her opinion, Jeffrey Dolan was the last man on earth ready for the Big C.

Lindsey hesitated, then asked, "How about you…and Jeffrey? Are you sure both of you are ready to make a commitment?"

For a moment Stephanie looked uncertain. Then, with a shake of her head, she said, "Jeffrey and I share the same goals. We want to build successful careers—I've joined his father's law firm, you know—and start our own family, right here in Whisper Key. Our life will be perfect. Just perfect."

Lindsey noted the adamant tone, the determined glint in her eye. Stephanie was a true counselor making her point. She wondered just who Stephanie was trying to convince of her case. Lindsey? Or herself?

"I hope you'll be happy," Lindsey murmured, chiding herself for letting the opportunity to tell Stephanie the truth—that her fiancé was a two-timing rat fink—slip through her hands. As much as she'd like to help Alex's sister, she just couldn't be the one to burst Stephanie's bubble of happiness. She knew all too well the pain caused by betrayal.

"We will be," Stephanie assured her.

An army of beauticians approached them. Talk of love and marriage went to the wayside of professional pampering. Their conversation lingered in Lindsey's mind, however, leaving her with a niggling sense of unease.

Since Danny's death, Alex had been faithful in his visits to her and Jamie. But Stephanie was wrong; loyalty and friendship had been his only motivations. It wasn't until this weekend that they'd begun noticing each other in a different way.

Wasn't it?

Her discomfort grew as she recalled the number of times Alex came calling, well after Jamie had been tucked into bed for the night. And all the phone calls he'd made, asking about Jamie, and how often the conversations steered to her. The look of concern in his eyes, and the gentle admonishment in his tone when he believed her to be overdoing it.

How blind could she be?

How long ago had Alex's feelings really changed? Two days? Two months? Or two years?

Lindsey frowned. If that were the case, then why in the world hadn't he said something to her before now?

Chapter Seven

From the last pew in church, Lindsey watched with a jaded eye as the wedding rehearsal unfolded before her. In these hallowed halls, Jeffrey stood in front of family and friends and carried off a mock rendition of his wedding vows. Her empty stomach roiled at his slick performance. He almost had her believing the sincerity in his tone.

A smiling Stephanie followed his lead.

No, no, no...Lindsey shouted a silent protest. After spending the day getting to know Stephanie, she truly liked Alex's sister. She didn't want to see her hurt.

Jeffrey represented everything that had gone wrong in Lindsey's own stab at wedded bliss. Despite all of the problems she and Danny had suffered, a part of her wanted to believe that there was such a thing as a faithful marriage. She couldn't allow this farce to happen.

The minister, a tall, lanky man, echoed her thoughts. "And then I'll ask the traditional, 'If there's anyone here who has just cause why this man and this woman should not be joined in holy wedlock, speak now or forever hold your peace.'''

Lindsey's heart leaped in her chest. Now was her chance. The opportunity she'd been waiting for. She felt herself rising from the pew. She opened her mouth to speak—

"Which of course, no one will answer," the minister added. His long, narrow face broke into a toothy grin. "I've been marrying couples for nigh on twenty years. I've yet to see a wedding where anyone has had the nerve to stop the ceremony."

A tittering of good-natured laughter met his proclamation.

Lindsey sank down onto the pew like a rock. Who was she kidding? A total stranger accusing the favored son-in-law-to-be with unfaithfulness? Without a shred of proof? Jeffrey had his innocent act down so pat, no one would believe her in a million years.

The minister's cheerful voice continued. "And then, I'll pronounce you husband and wife. Jeffrey, you will kiss your bride. Then you'll both turn to your guests, at which time I'll introduce you as Mr. and Mrs. Jeffrey Dolan."

The sick feeling just kept getting worse and worse. Lindsey swallowed hard at the bitterness rising in her throat. She likened the experience to a train barreling down at her in slow motion. She knew there was going to be certain disaster. But for the life of her, she just didn't know how to prevent it.

"Jeffrey, Stephanie, you'll be the first down the aisle…that's it. Best man, take the maid of honor's hand. Then big brothers, follow their lead. Perfect."

Alex, with a blushing bridesmaid clinging to his arm, made his way down the aisle. Lindsey felt her pulse

quicken when his blue-eyed gaze swept over her. In a
dark suit and tie, with his blond hair shimmering beneath
the chapel's lights, he looked devastatingly handsome.
When he smiled, she tingled beneath a full body flush,
one that she felt from the tips of her toes to the roots of
her hair.

Perhaps it was time she stopped worrying about
Stephanie and started worrying about herself. Like, how
she was going to get through an entire evening with Alex
at her side and not be tempted to throw herself at the
poor man.

Lindsey sighed. Whether it was the pampering at the
Pink Flamingo, or the pitcher of strawberry daiquiris she
and Stephanie had imbibed during the course of the afternoon, she felt more relaxed than she had in years.
Even her view on her situation with Alex had taken on
a new light.

Fretfulness had given way to resignation. So what if
she was the last person to know Alex was attracted to
her? She'd been under an extreme amount of stress as
of late. An elephant could have parked itself in her living
room and she probably wouldn't have noticed.

So, Alex's track record with women wasn't the best
in the world. A man could change, couldn't he?

What mattered was…Alex. In all the years she'd
known him, he'd yet to disappoint her. He'd been loyal
and reliable. He had never lied to her or misled her in
any way. She trusted him. She cared about him as a
friend. Perhaps it was only natural for the complexion
of that caring to change.

She took in a steadying breath and returned Alex's
smile.

Disentangling himself from the ardent bridesmaid,
Alex strode over to join her. "Ready to go?"

"Whenever you are," she said, ignoring the goose bumps his closeness caused.

He took her arm and Lindsey shivered beneath his touch. If he noticed, he was enough of a gentleman not to point out her reaction. "We're riding to the yacht club's rehearsal dinner with Jon."

"Fine," she murmured.

"So what did you think of the rehearsal?"

That it was the most hypocritical scene I'd ever witnessed, she screamed silently. "It was great, just great," she said, forcing an even tone.

He nodded, steering her through the church doors and into the quickly darkening parking lot.

Lindsey stopped, looking out to the west over the Gulf where the sun was in its final descent. From the palest of pinks to the deepest of reds, from royal purple to robin's egg blue, the sky was brushed with an array of hues. All of which left a shimmering reflection on the endless stretch of water.

"Oh, Alex. Isn't it beautiful?"

He followed the direction of her gaze, glancing at the skyline before turning his attention to her. A slow smile lit his face, a smile almost as breathtaking as the sunset.

"Yes," he said, his deep voice a quiver through her soul. "Beautiful."

Warning signals clanged in her head. Alex was a charmer. She shouldn't—couldn't—let herself fall under his spell of seduction. She stammered, "I, um, never realized just how wonderful a sunset could be."

"In Florida, everything seems perfect," he returned evenly, his gaze unwavering. Nothing but sincerity was reflected in his eyes.

Lindsey felt herself falling, and falling hard.

At that moment, time stopped. The world around them

ceased to exist. Their awareness of each other was all-encompassing. They stood at the edge of the parking lot, staring into each other's eyes.

"You two ready?" Jon asked, striding up to join them. He gave the car keys an impatient jangle, effectively breaking the spell. "Let's get out of here."

Flustered, Lindsey glanced around the nearly empty parking lot. How long had they stood gawking at each other? Seconds? Minutes? A lifetime? Her cheeks warmed with embarrassment. If this were any indication of how the climate of the evening would fare, she was headed for stormy weather.

Lindsey sat between Jon and Alex in the front seat of their mother's sedate Cadillac Seville. Jon's driving, however, was anything but calm. Palm trees, mimosas and beach houses flew by as they sped down the coastal highway. A sharp curve threw her against Alex, plastering her against his warm strength. If she weren't so scared, she'd have enjoyed the experience more.

"What the hell's the matter with you, Jon?" Alex growled. "Slow down before we end up in the Gulf."

Jon eased up on the gas, but his agitation remained in high gear. "Which way is it to the yacht club?"

"Head back to Mom and Dad's," Alex said. "It's just down the beach from their house."

The tension between the brothers was palpable.

Lindsey cleared her throat and lied, "The rehearsal seemed to go smoothly. I hope tomorrow's ceremony will go as well."

"You never know," Jon muttered gloomily. "Even the best laid plans have a way of going haywire."

Lindsey looked at Alex, transmitting a silent question with her eyes.

Alex shook his head and sighed. He narrowed a warning glance at Jon. "Cool down, big brother. Now isn't the time or the place for self-pity."

Jon snapped his fingers. "That's right, we're supposed to encourage Stephanie's illusion of happily-ever-after. She'll have to wait until after the ceremony to find out the truth...that all wedding vows are a sham." He gave a mirthless laugh. "In this day and age, there is no such thing as "till death do us part.""

A stunned silence echoed throughout the car.

Lindsey drew in a sharp breath, feeling as though she'd been slapped. ""Till death do us part." There couldn't have been a more accurate description of her own marriage's tragic end. But perhaps there was a glimmer of truth in Jon's dire prediction. If Danny hadn't died...

"For Pete's sake, Jon. That's the last thing Lindsey needs to hear," Alex rasped. He reached for her hand and squeezed it gently.

Jon swore softly beneath his breath, realization sinking in. "I'm sorry, Lindsey. I wasn't thinking. I didn't mean—"

"It's okay, Jon," she said quickly, wishing to forget the entire incident. "Obviously, something's wrong. You're upset. I know you didn't mean to say anything to hurt me."

Jon grimaced. "Jeez, Lindsey. The last thing I deserve is your understanding. I'd feel a whole lot better if you'd just take a poke at me."

His expression was so contrite, his tone so sincere, Lindsey couldn't help but smile. "Maybe later. Right now, I'd like to get to dinner in one piece."

Lindsey felt an easing of tension throughout the car, except in Alex. His muscles relaxed. The tension faded from his face. But he did not release the hold he'd had on her hand. His grip remained steady and reassuring.

Jon pulled into the parking lot of the Whisper Key Yacht Club and Lindsey felt a tug of disappointment. She could have spent an entire evening cocooned against the strength of Alex's warm body.

Alex opened the door and stepped outside.

Lindsey slid across the seat to join him. The air felt cool and moist against her skin, thick with the salty scent of the sea. Dusk had given way to night. Stars twinkled in the velvety sky. Despite her qualms about Stephanie's upcoming wedding, it had the makings of a perfect night.

Alex reclaimed Lindsey's hand and led her to the clubhouse. The gesture was possessive and totally unnecessary. But since his brother's callous remark, he felt oddly protective of Lindsey, unwilling to let her stray far from his side. Touching her, keeping her close, seemed as natural as breathing.

Crushed oyster shells crunched beneath their feet at the club's entrance. The white brick and glass building jutted out onto the water on a pier supported by large wood pilings. On three sides, it was surrounded by water, affording its guests a panoramic view of the Gulf.

Alex's family, the Dolans, and the rest of the wedding party converged in the opulent lobby.

Jeffrey's mother, a tall, elegantly coiffed woman, raised her voice to be heard over the din of excited voices. "Your attention, everyone." She waved a hand at the tuxedoed man standing next to her. "Henri tells me the private dining room is ready. If we'll all follow him, he'll show us the way."

With Lindsey at Alex's side, they joined the slow exodus into the dining room. Out of the corner of his eye, he noticed a man dressed in the white jacket of a waiter snag Stephanie's attention. Surreptitiously, the man handed her a plain manila envelope, shrugging in response to her questions. Murmuring something to Jeffrey, Stephanie slipped away from the group and headed for the ladies' room.

Trepidation shivered through him, unbidden like an omen of doom. For some unexplainable reason, he had the urge to follow his sister.

"Hey, are you okay?" Lindsey asked, drawing him out of his troubled thoughts.

Alex blinked. "Of course...I'm starved, that's all." He forced a smile. "All this sea air is making me hungry."

Her face lit up with an innocent smile that made his heart ache.

Apprehension soon gave way to a more pressing problem, undeniable awareness. Wanting Lindsey was becoming a life force of its own. He didn't know how he was going to get through the night without giving in to temptation. He didn't know if he had the strength to fight it.

Frosty glasses of champagne were served along with trays overflowing with appetizers. In between bites of crackers slathered with soft Brie, shrimp wrapped in pea pods and enough variety of fruit to tempt even Adam, Alex did his best to concentrate on making polite conversation. A hopeless task, he realized. With Lindsey so close, she was proving to be a formidable distraction.

Minutes passed and still there was no sign of Stephanie. Or Jeffrey, for that matter. Alex wasn't the only one to notice the happy couple's absence. His mother and Mrs. Dolan kept a watchful eye on the dining room's entrance. Finally, Alex's father was dispatched to gather up the wayward twosome.

Alex steered Lindsey over to join his parents, when his father came back empty-handed. Shrugging, he announced, "It seems Stephanie and Jeffrey have left the clubhouse."

"Left?" his mother repeated, her expression shocked. "How could they leave? This is their rehearsal dinner."

He shook his head. "I have no idea. The maître d' said they seemed to be having a rather intense discussion before disappearing out the front door."

A frown furrowed his mother's brow. "I don't like the sound of this."

"Neither do I," Mrs. Dolan agreed.

"Jeffrey's doing, no doubt." Mr. Dolan shook his head, his bulldog features stern. "Stephanie's such a positive influence. I'd hoped their marriage would settle the boy down."

"Any suggestions?" Mr. Trent raised a brow in question. "What do we do now?"

"Well, we can't have a rehearsal dinner without the bride and groom," his mother said.

Jon stepped up, joining the conversation. "Whisper Key isn't that big of an island. Want me to drive around, see if I can find them?"

"Would you?" Mrs. Dolan gave a grateful smile. "I'd appreciate it."

"No problem." Jon placed his untouched glass of champagne on the table.

Alex stopped his exit. "Need some help?"

Jon shook his head. "Stay here and help keep the party going. I won't be long."

Lindsey pulled Alex aside. "Alex, I've got a bad feeling about this."

Alex looked down at her. Not wanting his own unease to spoil her evening, he forced a smile. "I'm sure it's nothing to worry about. Stephanie and Jeffrey are getting married tomorrow. They probably just need a little time alone."

"Yes, but—"

"But nothing. I know my sister. She can take care of herself." He chucked a finger beneath her chin, grazing the satiny smoothness of her skin. "She's fine, really."

Lindsey frowned. "If you're sure—"

"I'm positive." Unable to stop himself, he placed a hand around her shoulder and pulled her close. A mistake, for sure. Heat surged through his body. He feigned a lighthearted tone. "Now stop worrying about Stephanie, and start worrying about the shrimp. Let's grab some before the maid-of-honor scoffs down the last tray."

Forty-five minutes later, there was still no sign of the guests of honor. Mr. Dolan and one of Jeffrey's cousins had joined the search party. The tension in the room was so thick, it was palpable.

Alex felt the tension, all right. But his unease had nothing to do with anxiety over the missing couple and everything to do with Lindsey.

Still firmly at his side, her soft body curved snugly against his hard strength. Their combined body heat had raised the room temperature by at least twenty degrees. Her delicate perfume surrounded him, making him dizzy, making his empty stomach growl with hunger.

The appetizers had disappeared twenty minutes ago, leaving them with nothing but champagne to guzzle. After his third glass of bubbly, his inhibitions were flying at an all-time low. Wisely, Alex passed on the next round of drinks.

"They're not coming back," Mrs. Trent said flatly.

"What do you suggest we do now?" his father asked, trying unsuccessfully to hide his concern.

"Well, we can't keep telling everyone Stephanie's powdering her nose. They stopped believing that line half an hour ago." Mrs. Dolan sighed. "There's nothing we can do but tell them the truth. The party's over."

Mrs. Trent patted the other woman's arm. "I'll take care of it, Alice."

As his father tapped the rim of his champagne glass with a shrimp fork, drawing everyone's attention, Alex leaned close and whispered in Lindsey's ear, "Let's get out of here."

His lips brushed the smooth skin of her neck, sending shock waves of awareness tripping throughout him.

She shivered beneath his touch. "How? We came with Jon."

Alex shrugged. "It isn't that far. We could walk home."

"What about Stephanie? Your parents?" There was just a slight breathless quality to her voice, as though she were afraid.

Afraid of him? He didn't blame her. The way his hormones were raging, he didn't trust himself, either.

Nervously, she licked her lips. "Shouldn't we try to help?"

"Help them with what?" he asked with only a touch of impatience. "Until Stephanie and Jeffrey resurface, there isn't anything anyone can do."

She didn't look convinced.

Alex gave a resigned breath. "Look, I'll talk to my mother. If she wants us to stay, then we will."

As soon he left her side, he felt an instant chill. He missed the soft warmth of her body. While striding purposefully to his parents, he kept a watchful eye on Lindsey. Curiously, she grabbed a fluted champagne glass off a passing waiter's tray and took a hefty swig of the drink. Her cheeks were flushed by the time Alex returned.

"We've been given the green light. My mother says she'll let us know if there's anything else we can do." Alex placed a hand at the small of her back. He frowned as he felt her stiffen beneath his touch. "Ready to go?"

Hesitantly, she nodded.

They used the side exit, which emptied out onto the beach, circumventing the crowd at the entrance. Moonlight cascaded down onto the water, bathing the night in a soft glow. The air felt cool, refreshing against his skin.

Lindsey shivered, wrapping her arms around her waist. Her dress was black and cap-sleeved. It dipped low in the front, exposing a healthy expanse of enticing skin. A fact that hadn't escaped his attention during the entire evening. Reluctant to hide such a perfect example of the female body, but ever-mindful of his manners, he shrugged off his jacket and slipped it over her shoulders. His hands lingered on the lapels.

"Thank you," she said, her teeth chattering.

He smiled. "The Florida sunshine has spoiled you. What are you going to do when you get back to the frosty Midwest?"

"Freeze," she admitted, grinning up at him.

Her strawberry-colored lips looked ripe and full, tempting enough to nibble on. The thought brought a new wave of awareness crashing down upon him. His breath caught. His body tightened. He'd never needed a woman more than he did Lindsey. He ached with wanting her.

Clearing his throat, he said, "Well, there's nothing I

can do about that now." Slowly, he slid his hands to her shoulders, ready to pull her close. "Perhaps, there's something we can do about warming you up now."

"M-maybe walking will help," she stammered, her eyes wide and uncertain.

Not bothering to hide his disappointment, Alex released her. "Yeah, that might do the trick."

Wordlessly, they headed for the house. An uneasy silence stretched between them.

A few feet into the walk, Lindsey wobbled to stop. "This isn't going to work. Heels and sand don't mix." Supporting herself against his chest with one hand, she used the other to slide her heels off her feet. With a smile of pure delight, she dug her silken-clad toes into the sand and sighed. "Ah...much better."

Alex shook his head. One minute, she seemed as timid as an innocent. The next, she was as wild and carefree as a vixen. Whichever the case might be, the woman was driving him crazy.

"Let's go," he said, his voice gruff, revealing more impatience than he'd intended.

The light faded from her beautiful smile. Clutching her shoes against her breasts, she hurried to keep up with his long-legged stride. "Sure," she sighed. "Whatever you want, Alex."

The words brought him careening to a stop. Looking her straight in the eye, he said, "Be careful what you promise, Lindsey. You might be surprised at what I want."

She swallowed hard, looking as though she were fighting a personal battle of courage. "Maybe it's time you told me exactly what it is you do want, Alex."

He stared at her for a long moment. Then, without a word, he made his message clear. Reaching for her, he pulled her roughly into his arms. His mouth came down upon hers and he took what had been long denied.

He tasted of champagne, breath mints and a taste that could only be Alex. A taste that was exactly what she'd been craving. Greedily, Lindsey parted her lips and sought more.

Alex did not argue.

His mouth was warm, firm, and anything but gentle. His tongue was quick and thorough. He raked his fingers through her hair and angled her head for easier access. Her body pulsed as he plundered her mouth.

With a single touch, Alex had opened the floodgates on a deluge of long pent-up emotions. Once released, she knew she could no longer deny these feelings. She couldn't remember the last time, if ever, she'd experienced such an overwhelming desire. Her body felt weak with wanting him.

Her shoes fell from her hands, thudding softly against the sand. She lifted a hand to stroke his face. Her fingertips tingled at the contrast of smooth skin and the roughness of his late-day beard.

Restlessly, blindly in the darkness, she sought the rest of him. She felt the heat of his body through the fabric of his shirt. She sculpted the unrelenting hardness of his shoulders. And fitted her palms alongside the narrowness of his hips.

He crushed her soft curves against his hard body and she felt the full force of his desire.

His jacket slipped from her shoulders. She shivered in the cool night air. His hands, then his lips, covered her bare skin, warding off the chill and setting her on fire.

Sucking in a draft of bracing air, she demanded, "How far away is the house?"

"Too far," he muttered, claiming her mouth once again.

Voices sounded in the distance, reminding them they were not alone.

"Alex," she whispered, pulling away. "I really think we should go back to the house."

He growled his frustration, but did not argue.

Picking up the discarded shoes and the forgotten jacket, they slowly made their way back to the house, stopping often to quench their newfound thirst for each other. By the time they reached the veranda their bodies hummed with desire.

Alex fumbled with the key in the lock of his bedroom's patio door. It seemed like an eternity before the door clicked open and they stumbled inside. Letting the moonlight be their guide, they crossed the room to the bed, dropping shoes and loosening clothes as they went.

At the foot of the bed, they stopped, catching their breaths as they stared at each other. Alex's shirt was unbuttoned, her dress unzipped. His hair looked tousled and sexy. She wondered if her eyes were as wide and blazed with as much desire as his.

Passion roared in her ears, competing with the sea breaking outside, drowning out any lingering thoughts of caution. Slowly she lifted her hands to his shoulders and slid his shirt out of her way. She raked her fingers over the smooth muscles of his chest and felt his shuddering breath when her lips followed.

A primal growl of desire rose in his throat. With an animal quickness, her dress hit the floor and Lindsey found herself being lifted off her feet and placed on the bed. The mattress dipped beneath their weight as he joined her.

"You are beautiful," he said, showering butterfly

kisses across her lips, her chin, her neck. With the tips of his fingers, he traced a path to the hollow of her breasts. "I want to touch and taste every inch of you."

His breath felt warm, tickling her as he lowered his mouth and kissed the swell of one lace-clad breast, then the other. Goose bumps skittered across her skin. Liquid heat blossomed inside her, sending petals of desire coursing through her body.

Silently, guiltily, she'd acknowledged that even in the best of moments to her marriage with Danny she had never felt such an intensity of emotions. With a touch of his lips and a caress of his hand, Alex had evoked in her a desire so powerful, she felt as though she might shatter beneath its weight.

She dug her fingers through the thick curls of hair at the back of his head. Tugging gently, she lifted his face so that she could see his eyes, those beautiful, blue eyes. She told him the words she knew he needed to hear. "I want you, Alex. I want you to make love to me. I want you to make me feel alive again."

He released a shaky breath. "You don't know how long I've waited for you to say those words."

Then he claimed her lips in another long and searing kiss.

She tore her mouth from his, reveling in the knowledge that she was desired. Playfully, she ran her fingernails down the sinewy strength of his back. Smiling, she whispered, "How long?"

The world stopped spinning when, without a moment's hesitation, he answered, "Since the day I met you."

Chapter Eight

"W-what did you say?" Lindsey's hand stilled at the small of his back.

Alex muttered a quiet oath, cursing his newfound honesty.

She gave a nervous laugh. "Alex, we've known each other a long time."

Thankful for the darkness, he felt his skin warm with discomfort. He swallowed hard, not trusting himself to speak. He'd never felt closer to Lindsey. The moment was ripe for confessions. But he'd revealed enough of his feelings as it was. Telling a woman he wanted her was one thing. Admitting that he was in love with her— at least, not until he knew for certain his feelings were returned—was the last thing he needed to do.

"Hmm..." he growled, nuzzling her earlobe, breathing in her sweet scent, hoping to distract her long enough to forget his slip of the tongue.

She cupped his face in both of her hands, stopping his

diversionary tactics and forcing him to look at her. "Alex, why haven't you said anything to me before?"

He shrugged. "The time never seemed right."

"Never seemed right?" She released him and pushed herself to her elbows. A painfully clear emotion flickered across her face. Lindsey was irritated. "Let me get this straight. You've been...attracted to me for—for years, but you've never found the right time to tell me?"

"Lindsey, when I first met you, you were too young. And I was too old," he said, determined to remain calm in the wake of her unwarranted agitation. "Your father was a policeman. Have you ever heard the term jail-bait?"

She gave an exasperated breath. "I grew up, Alex. I turned eighteen. What stopped you then?"

"Lots of reasons," he said, frowning at the vague-sounding excuse. Somehow, worshiping Lindsey from afar sounded much more romantic in practice than in theory. "I was getting my M.B.A., you left for college. I thought there'd be plenty of time. But..."

"But—what?"

He swallowed hard. "But then you started seeing Danny."

"Danny," she murmured, sitting up.

Alex shivered, missing the warmth of her body next to his. He felt as though he were losing her before they'd even had a chance to be together. Perhaps now wasn't the right time to bring Danny into the conversation. But if he didn't, Danny's memory would forever stand between them.

"Danny was my best friend, Lindsey. He trusted me. I couldn't..." Alex sighed. "I wouldn't have done anything to break his faith in me."

Lindsey nodded. She averted her gaze, turning her

back on him. Her shoulders shuddered as she sucked in a deep breath. "You're telling me you've felt this way…you've wanted me, all this time?"

"Yes," he said, reaching out to her.

She flinched as his fingers grazed the silky-smooth skin of her shoulders. He pulled back, feeling wounded by her reaction. Her voice barely a whisper, she said, "Danny's gone, Alex. He's been gone for over two years."

"I know that—"

She looked at him, emotion flashing in her eyes. "For someone supposedly pining away for me, you've certainly kept yourself busy with other women."

The cool anger in her tone stunned him. "Lindsey, it isn't what you think—"

"It's exactly what I think." She scrambled off the bed, gathering her clothes as she went. "We're not talking about a few women in your life, Alex. We're talking about dozens. Maybe more."

"Don't be ridiculous," he said, his defenses kicking in. "There haven't been that many women."

"Ha!" She picked up one of her shoes, brandishing it like a sword. "Who are you trying to kid, Alex? You might as well have installed a revolving door in your bedroom. It certainly would have made their comings and goings that much easier."

Alex winced at the barb. In her current frame of mind, he didn't think she'd be open to the drowning-his-sorrows-in-female-companionship explanation. Nor did he think she'd believe him if he told her the truth. That he'd cared too much, that he'd rather live his life as only her friend, than risk the pain of her rejection.

He pushed himself from the bed, determination spurring him on. Okay, so she hadn't reacted to the news as well as he'd hoped, that didn't mean he was going to give up. He'd waited too long for this moment. He wasn't going to blow it now.

"Lindsey, honey—"

"Don't you 'honey' me, Alex Hale Trent," she said, backing away, holding her dress in front of her like a shield.

He gritted his teeth against the flash of impatience. "Lindsey, be reasonable. I can explain—"

"I don't want to hear any excuses. I'm sure I've heard them all before."

Heard them all before? He felt confused. His heart clenched at the trembling sound of her voice. Her eyes glittered in the moonlight, filling with unshed tears. Somehow he'd hurt her. Perhaps, irrevocably.

"Lindsey, I'm sorry—"

She kicked a pillow out of her way. "You know, if I had a nickel for every time a man has told me he was sorry, I'd be a wealthy woman by now."

Alex was more confused than ever. He had a funny feeling they weren't just talking about him…about the here and now. Lindsey was showing all the signs of a woman who'd been hurt deeply. And not just by his hesitancy in telling her the truth…that he'd fallen in love with her.

She found her other shoe. Scooping it up, she headed for the door adjoining her bedroom.

Panic seized him. He couldn't let her go. Not yet. Not like this, angry and upset. He reached out, grabbing her arm to stop her. Her skin felt hot, sizzling beneath his touch.

"Lindsey, wait," he said, his voice a quiet plea for understanding.

"I think I've waited long enough, Alex." She jerked

her arm from his grasp. "If you were serious about this…this attraction to me, you'd have done something about it long before now."

"Lindsey, you don't mean that—"

"Oh, yes, I do, Alex," she said, her voice quivering with emotion. A tear slid down her cheek, shimmering wetly in the moonlight. "I refuse to have a fling with a man who's unable to make a commitment. It just hurts too damn much."

She left him then. Without another word, she spun on her heel and escaped through the door adjoining their bedrooms.

Click…the sound of the lock sliding home reverberated throughout the room.

Click…the noise echoed in his ears, striking like a hammer against his heart.

Click…the sound of Lindsey shutting him out.

Years of frustration churned inside him, slowly turning to anger. Something deep inside him snapped. He teetered on the edge of control. The urge to break down the door and force her to listen to reason overwhelmed him. He cared too much to let her go without a fight.

In two quick steps, he made short the distance between him and the door. Until, with his hand on the knob, he heard the soft, muffled sobs. Lindsey was crying.

Alex leaned his forehead against the door and closed his eyes against the sound. The door felt cold against his skin, as hard and unrelenting as the throbbing in his chest. Bullying her wasn't the answer. He'd caused her enough pain for one night. It was time to back off, give her some time to reconsider.

He'd waited over ten years for this moment, he told himself, a little longer wouldn't hurt.

Opening his eyes, Alex pushed himself away from the door. He flicked on the switch, turning on the bedside lamp. Then wished he hadn't. The rumpled bedcovers caught his eye. Clearly, he could see two indentations side by side on the bed, his and Lindsey's.

Images of their thwarted lovemaking flashed in his mind. He snapped off the light, refusing to allow the thought to go any further. Grabbing his clothes from the floor, he dressed quickly in the darkness.

He'd told Lindsey that he'd wanted her. That his feelings for her were not fleeting. Yet she'd reacted as though he'd proposed an illicit affair.

Alex set his jaw against a niggling of unease that perhaps she was right. That, perhaps, if he'd really wanted to make a commitment to her, then he'd have done so by now. That nothing, not school, not work, not even the memory of his best friend would have stood in his way. Stubbornly, he refused to acknowledge his own culpability in this confusing turn of events.

He glanced at the disorderly room. Of one thing he was certain: he couldn't stay here tonight. The memories of holding Lindsey in his arms would never let him rest.

Unable to shake the feeling that he was running away, Alex stepped out into the hallway and gave a ragged sigh of relief. He pushed a hand through his tousled hair and glared at Lindsey's closed door.

He'd made a real mess of things tonight. Dammit, he needed a drink.

A solitary drink, however, wasn't in the cards.

"Stephanie, darling." Mrs. Trent's voice held a quiet plea for cooperation. "Can't you just tell us what's wrong?"

The Trent family was gathered in the living room.

Alex had been the last to join the meeting of the clan. Minutes ago, when he'd staggered in for a much-needed drink and a few blessed moments of peace and quiet, he knew he'd been dealt an appropriate end to a perfectly rotten night.

Cradling a glass of Scotch in his hand, he waited for Stephanie's answer. He felt as though he'd been dropped into an episode of Ozzie and Harriet gone awry. Nah, he told himself, there never would have been as much tears and theatrics in TV land.

His protective instincts kicked into high gear as he watched his sister wipe a tissue beneath her eyes. Dressed in a taupe sheath dress, with three-inch heels on her feet and her blond hair twisted into a sophisticated knot at the back of her head, she looked like a kid playing dress-up in her mother's clothes. To him, she'd always be his baby sister.

"The wedding's off, Mother," Stephanie said, gathering her poise.

Big surprise, Alex mused. Everyone had gathered as much hours ago, when she and Jeffrey pulled a no-show for their rehearsal dinner.

"But why, darling?" his mother asked.

"And where have you been all evening?" Mr. Trent piped in. "Our guests were waiting for you and Jeffrey at the yacht club. Couldn't you have let someone know what was happening?"

"I'm sorry, Daddy." Stephanie rolled her eyes, fresh tears escaping. "I was just a little bit busy."

"Doing what?" Mr. Trent demanded. "And where? We had search parties looking for you, young lady."

From his spot on the couch, Jon cleared his throat, trying his best not to smile. "I, um, found them at the public beach on Coconut Drive."

"The public beach?" Mrs. Trent looked confused. "Darling, the yacht club's smack-dab in the middle of the ocean. If you wanted to walk on the beach, why didn't you stay a little closer to home?"

Jon came to her defense. "I don't think she had a choice, Mom."

"Jeffrey kidnapped me," Stephanie explained. "The rat insisted we talk in private. But when I wanted to leave, he refused to take me back to the party."

Mrs. Trent's brow furrowed; worry lines etched her face. "Darling, that's terrible. Jeffrey has always been such a fine young man, I can't imagine—"

"He wasn't happy, Mother," Stephanie said, impatience edging out the tears. "Things weren't going his way. I'd finally found out his true colors—the skunk!"

"Stephanie, please," Mr. Trent said, his tone cautious. "I realize you're upset. And we're trying to understand. If you could just tell us what happened..."

Stephanie swallowed hard, averting her eyes. "To put it bluntly, Jeffrey hasn't been all that faithful. He's been seeing other women while we've been engaged."

Alex flinched. Lindsey's lack of confidence in his own integrity was a fresh and vivid memory in his mind. The unjustness of her accusations—that he'd never be able to make a commitment—still had him brooding over the fickle-heartedness of women. He shifted uncomfortably, hating to acknowledge even a remote kindredship to Jeffrey.

"Are you sure?" their mother asked, drawing Alex out of his self-pitying thoughts.

"Am I sure?" Stephanie gave a bitter laugh. "I'm positive, Mother. I have the eight-by-ten glossies to prove it. An anonymous friend kindly sent them to me tonight, during my rehearsal dinner. They were waiting for me at the yacht club.''

The envelope, Alex realized. His instincts were right. Stephanie had been in trouble at the rehearsal dinner. He should have followed his heart and sought her out.

His grip tightened around the rim of his Scotch glass. There was no comparison between his situation with Lindsey and what Jeffrey had done to his sister. If Lindsey had agreed to be his wife, all other women would be a vague and distant memory. His faithfulness to her would not be a question.

''Stephanie, maybe it's not what you think—''

''For Pete's sake, Mother. I've got a wide-angle shot of Jeffrey necking on *our* veranda with my *former* best friend at our *engagement party*.''

''Oh, dear,'' his mother mumbled.

Alex slammed his glass onto the coffee table and surged to his feet. ''Where is this guy?''

Jon rose to meet him, placing a staying hand on his shoulder. ''Don't bother, brother. Stephanie already took care of the weasel.'' Jon grinned. ''By the time I found the pair, Jeffrey was sporting a fat lip and a swollen eye. Our hellcat of a sister had whacked him with her purse when Jeffrey had refused to drive her home.''

Alex looked at his sister with undisguised admiration. Stubbornly, daring him to show even the slightest bit of pity, she met his gaze head-on.

At that moment he knew Stephanie would be all right. Being the brunt of two older brothers' jokes and constant teasing had toughened up their little sister. It would take a lot more than a man like Jeffrey Dolan to bring her down.

''Goodness, you certainly can't marry him now. He doesn't deserve you, Stephanie,'' his mother announced firmly. Then, with a sorrowful shake of her head, she tsk-tsked. "Though I have to admit, I am a little disappointed. I had hoped to have two children happily married by the end of this weekend. Now, I still only have one."

Jon pivoted on one foot and made a hasty retreat to the bar. With a grim look on his face, he poured himself two fingers of whisky, downing it in one gulp.

Alex lowered himself back into his seat on the couch and waited for the next round of fireworks to begin.

"Mom, Dad," Jon began. "I have something to tell you."

They looked at him—their oldest son, their Golden Boy, the one who could do no wrong—with expectant glances.

Jon took a deep breath and blurted, "Rachel and I are having a few problems. We've separated."

"Oh, Jon." Their mother sagged against the back of her chair. "Not you, too."

Their father placed a supporting hand on her shoulder. "Is it serious, Jon?"

Jon rubbed a weary hand across his face. "Yeah, Dad. It's serious."

"What's wrong with this family?" their mother moaned. "Why can't anyone settle down?" She fixed a gaze on Alex, a painfully obvious look in her eye. "Of course, there's still hope." She smiled. "Lindsey is such a sweet girl, Alex."

Alex squirmed beneath her gaze. If his mother only knew what a mess he'd made of the relationship between him and Lindsey, she wouldn't be hanging her hopes too highly upon him. "Mom, now isn't a good time—"

"That's right, Mother," Stephanie said, wobbling to her feet. "We should be applauding Alex for his good sense in not falling for the marriage trap. Live the good life, single and uncommitted, Alex. Don't let yourself be vulnerable to some two-timing rat fink.''

The bitterness in her voice hit him like a blow. He'd spent most of his life being the one who fixed problems, not caused them. A discomfitting wave of helplessness washed over him. His sister was in pain. And there wasn't a damn thing he could do about it.

Despite everything, a part of him didn't want to agree with her. The part that loved Lindsey with all his heart. He couldn't just give up on her. No matter how frustrating it might be. No matter how much it might hurt.

With a muffled sob, Stephanie hurried from the room. The rest of the Trent family rose to their feet.

Alex lifted a staying hand.

"Let me talk to her. If the whole family descends upon her, it'll just make it worse."

Reluctantly, his mother nodded. "All right, Alex." She narrowed a glance at Jon. "Besides, we need a little time alone with your brother. There's a lot we need to discuss."

Jon shot him a glance that had *help* written all over it.

Shaking his head, Alex strode from the room. Glad, for once, not to be on the receiving end of one of their mother's infamous lectures.

The next morning, sunlight poured in through the windows, warming her bedroom. Yet Lindsey felt chilled to the bone. Gloomily, she listened to the waves crashing against the shoreline. Her head throbbed with each and every undulation. A soft breeze wafted in from the open patio doors, bringing with it the fresh scent of the sea. She barely noticed.

It had the earmarks of a beautiful Saturday morning, a perfect day for a wedding.

Too bad she wouldn't be attending.

Lindsey glanced at her wristwatch. After a sleepless night, she'd risen at the crack of dawn and had called the airline to change her flight. In less than two hours she'd be on her way home…where she belonged.

Sighing, she stuffed her makeup kit into her suitcase and slammed the lid shut. If she were lucky, she'd be long gone before Alex realized she'd even left.

Alex. Her hand caught on the suitcase latch. Thoughts of him had kept her awake the entire evening. No matter how hard she'd tried not to, her mind had replayed over and over again what had happened between them last night.

She doubted if she'd ever forget how it felt to be held in his arms. To have his lips on her skin, touching her, tasting her, setting her on fire.

Lindsey sighed again. She knew her reaction hadn't been rational. But last night, what had happened with Alex had reminded her so much of Danny.

Danny and Alex were alike in so many ways. They were both handsome, sweet-talking charmers. By using their powers of persuasion, they could see their way out of any sticky situation. Countless times, Danny had lied straight to her face, and she'd been none the wiser. He'd broken her heart. If she allowed Alex to get close, would he do the same? Would she ever be able to trust him with her heart?

A light knock sounded on the door.

Like a deer caught in the headlights, Lindsey froze. She gulped in a deep, bracing draft of air, chiding herself for not leaving earlier.

"Lindsey?"

Her pulse quickened as she heard his voice. He sounded as tired and as miserable as she felt. She couldn't help but respond. "Just a moment."

Without thinking, she smoothed a hand over her hair. She licked her lips and glanced in the mirror. Then stopped, stunned by her actions. Since when did she care so much how she looked in front of Alex? A stupid question, she told herself, rolling her eyes, since he'd kissed her senseless the night before.

Steeling herself, she opened the door.

Still dressed in last night's rumpled clothes, his hair tousled, his eyes bloodshot, his beard unshaven, Alex looked like he'd been through hell and back. It took all of her willpower not to reach out, pull him into her arms and comfort him.

Skirting temptation, she wrapped her arms around her waist and studied him warily.

"May I come in?" he asked.

She bit her lip and mulled over the question. Despite all the pain and misery he'd caused her last night, she couldn't help but feel the tug of desire whenever she looked into his eyes. She wasn't sure if she trusted him...if she trusted herself to be alone with him, yet.

At her hesitancy, he narrowed a stern glance. "Lindsey, I need to talk to you. I'd just as soon this conversation be a private one. But if you insist, I'll be glad to discuss what happened between us last night wherever you'd like."

Lindsey stared at him, clinging to the door for protection. He sounded so strange, so different from the usually calm and collected Alex.

"Here would be fine," he said. There was an almost maniacal, out-of-control glint in his blue eyes as he swept a hand down the hall. "Or perhaps you'd rather go downstairs and join my family in the kitchen. I'm sure our sex life would make an entertaining breakfast topic.''

"Sex life?" Lindsey squeaked, finding her voice. Mortified, she grabbed him by his arm, pulled him inside and slammed the door closed behind him. She pointed a shaky finger at him. "You're crazy. Do you know that?"

"Yeah, I'm crazy about you," he sighed, catching her hand in his. He brought it to his lips, nibbling on her fingertips. His words, as well as his actions, sent a quivering of awareness throughout her limbs.

She snatched her hand away, beating a hasty retreat on legs that felt like jelly. "Alex, I told you last night—"

"I know what you told me, Lindsey. That's why I'm here. We have to talk. I need to explain a few things."

"I'm not in the mood for any explanations." She continued her retreat, backing away, with Alex in close pursuit. He looked wild and dangerous. He smelled of the sand and the sea. She also caught a whiff of alcohol. Her eyes widened. "Have you been drinking?"

He smiled, revealing a dazzling amount of even, white teeth. "Not nearly enough."

Her heel caught on the edge of the bedspread, knocking her off balance. She landed on her fanny on the bed, beside her suitcase.

Alex's smile faded. He glared at the suitcase. "What the hell is that?"

For just a moment Lindsey felt a fluttering of trepidation in the pit of her stomach. The Alex she knew was calm, dependable and reasonable. The Alex standing in front of her now was emotional, reckless, and more than a little unpredictable. Who knew what he might do next?

With a confidence she didn't feel, she lifted her chin and met his stormy gaze. "Don't be silly, Alex. It's a suitcase."

A disbelieving look crossed his face. "You're leaving?"

Her mouth went dry, feeling as though it had been filled with cotton. She swallowed hard. "My flight leaves in two hours."

"You weren't going to tell me?" The words were spoken slowly, calmly. But the look in his eye sent a shiver down her spine. Alex was not pleased.

She gave a nervous laugh. "Of course, I was going to tell you. I left you a note."

His gaze searched the room, stopping on a sheet of paper that rested on the nightstand. Striding to the nightstand in two quick steps, he snatched up the note and scanned the words. "Alex, I'm sorry I had to miss the wedding. But I am needed at home. Lindsey."

He fixed an angry look on her face. "Is Jamie sick?"

"No—"

"Did the house catch on fire?"

"Well, no—"

"Did your brother try to punch out another of the mayor's relatives?"

She straightened her shoulders, flashing him an indignant glance. "Of course not—"

Sparks of emotion danced in his blue eyes. "Then what was so damn important that you couldn't wait one more day?"

Crossing her arms across her chest, she remained stubbornly mute.

He set his jaw in a firm line. "You want to leave? Then fine. I'm going with you."

He slapped the note back onto the nightstand and headed for his own bedroom.

Lindsey jumped to her feet. "Y-you can't!"

"It's a free country, Lindsey," he tossed over his shoulder, not breaking stride. He paused at the door adjoining their bedrooms, that wild, unpredictable look still in place. "My comings and goings are no one's business but my own...as you so kindly pointed out last night."

Her face flamed with embarrassment. The cad! How dare he use her own angry words against her? "Alex, you can't leave now. What about your sister's wedding?"

Alex flinched at the question. The bravado faded from his stance. Concern flickered, then died in his eyes. In a flat, almost emotionless voice, he said, "There won't be a wedding today. The bride has had second thoughts."

Chapter Nine

An hour and forty-five minutes later, Alex stood waiting to board the airplane to St. Louis. Among the last in line, he felt dead on his feet. He hadn't slept at all last night.

He gave a tired sigh. After spending a grueling night consoling his mother and calming his baby sister, the thought of climbing into a big, soft bed had sounded mighty inviting. Only, Lindsey had had other plans. Rubbing a weary hand over his freshly shaven jaw, he narrowed a scowling glance at the woman standing in front of him.

With her back to him, her posture ramrod straight and her shoulders stiff beneath the folds of her tweed jacket, Lindsey looked a picture of self-righteous indignation. She hadn't spoken a word to him since sharing the ride to the airport. Even then it had been a sharp "I don't need any help, thank you" when he'd tried to take her suitcase.

Unable to stop himself, he lowered his gaze, taking in

her snug pair of jeans, her curvy backside and her long legs. Desire kicked him square in the gut. Alex scowled. Who was he kidding? He might as well be wishing for the moon. At the moment the lady would just as soon deck him than look at him.

The line moved. Lindsey showed her boarding pass to the flight attendant and stepped through the gate. Alex followed closely behind.

He watched as she kept one eye on her ticket, the other on the overhead seat numbers. She stopped at a seat one row in front of and one seat across the aisle from his own. Alex clenched and unclenched his fists in frustration. Since Lindsey had called hours before he had to change flights, he'd been unable to get the seat next to hers.

He waited for her to stow her purse under the seat before squatting in the aisle next to her. "We still need to talk."

Behind him, a woman cleared her throat, reminding him that he was blocking traffic.

Color rose on Lindsey's cheeks. Her brown eyes flashed with irritation. "Alex, now isn't the time."

"You wouldn't talk to me at the house. Or during the car ride over. Or in the airport. When exactly would be a good time?"

He hadn't meant the words to be so loud, or so harsh. Heads turned. Fellow travelers eyed them curiously.

Lindsey slunk lower in her seat.

The woman behind him tapped him on the shoulder. She was an older woman with graying hair and a fragile bone structure. She pointed a bony finger at the vacant seat next to Lindsey. "Young man, that's my seat you're keeping me from."

Alex sighed, rising to his feet. "Sorry, ma'am. I just needed to speak to my...friend."

The word seemed to stick in his throat. He wasn't sure if he had the right to still call Lindsey a friend. After last night, he wasn't sure of anything.

"Where are you sitting?" the woman demanded.

Alex pointed to the seat across the aisle. "Right there, ma'am."

The woman narrowed a sharp glance at him. "I suppose you think I'm going to offer you my seat, so's you can sit next to your friend?"

Alex blinked, looking expectantly at his savior, unable to believe his change in luck.

"Well, I'm not," she said bluntly. Scowling, she added, "I bought this ticket well in advance just so I could have a window seat. Now, move along, young man. You're in my way."

Lindsey snickered.

Alex shot her a quelling glance, but did as he was bid. He slung himself into his seat next to a young mother with a whimpering baby, clearing the way for the remaining passengers. His kneecap cracked against the seat in front of him, sending a sharp pain up his thigh. Mindful of the child nearby, he bit back an oath and rubbed the aching spot.

Lindsey stole a glance at him from across the aisle.

He gritted his teeth and forced a smile.

Raising her pert nose, she snapped her head back to the front of the airplane, feigning a sudden interest in the flight attendant's safety instructions.

The baby next to him fussed in her mother's lap. She waved her bottle in exasperation, sending a spray of formula shooting across his navy blue polo shirt.

Alex glanced at the mess and sighed. Oh, yeah, his

luck was changing, all right. All of it for the worse. If he survived the flight home, it would be a miracle.

The plane shimmied across the tarmac, lifting off without a hitch. Feeling tired and grumpy, Alex leaned back in his seat, ignored the crying baby, and fell promptly asleep. He didn't wake up until three hours later when the plane began its descent pattern into St. Louis.

A hand rested lightly on his shoulder. "Sir, please return your seat to an upright position."

The flight attendant moved on before Alex could blink his eyes into focus. Next to him, the baby gurgled and gave him a toothless grin. The harried young mother smiled wanly. Things, it would seem, were improving.

From her seat in front of him, Lindsey shot him a frosty glare.

Alex sighed. Or, maybe not. The plane bumped to an uneven stop. Alex stood, in a hurry to catch Lindsey before she had a chance to escape. The young mother remained seated, struggling with the baby and a recalcitrant diaper bag wedged beneath her seat.

Alex hesitated, watching Lindsey disappear down the aisle. Then, with a sigh, he turned to the young mother and asked, "Could I help?"

The mother gave a grateful smile. "Oh, yes. Thank you."

She handed him the baby.

The baby girl eyed him warily. She was warm and cuddly, as light as a feather. But there was a strong odor clinging to her little body, and she felt damp in all the wrong places.

Relief poured through him when the mother stood and reclaimed her bundle of joy. Murmuring a polite good-bye, Alex hurried down the aisle, bent on finding Lindsey. He didn't catch up with her until they neared the baggage claim carousel.

"You're going to have to talk to me eventually," he said, sidling up next to her.

She shifted her carry-on bag, angling it between them, refusing to look at him. "Not if I can at all help it."

He blew out a frustrated breath. "Could you at least tell me why you're so angry?"

"If you have to ask, then you'll never understand," she said, keeping her eyes focused straight ahead.

He gritted his teeth. Then, glancing at the crowd milling about them, he leaned close and whispered, "I told you I was attracted to you...that I've been attracted to you for a long time. What's so bad about that? Most women would be flattered."

"Well, I'm not most women."

He snorted. "That's for sure."

She glanced at him sharply. "What is that supposed to mean?"

"Nothing, just..."

"Just what?"

He sighed. "Lindsey, Danny's been gone for two years. You haven't been with any other men during that time. Your experience is...well, limited. It isn't any wonder that you'd be frightened—"

"You think I'm scared? Of men?"

"Well—"

She narrowed her eyes. "What makes you think I haven't been with any other men?"

His heart skipped a beat. He set his chin in a stubborn line and, unheedful of his jealous tone, demanded, "You haven't, have you?"

Lindsey rolled her eyes. "Alex, you're hopeless."

Bags began rolling down the conveyor belt.

"What do you mean, hopeless?"

She shook her head and gave a mirthless laugh. "I mean you, of all people, worrying about my morality."

Lindsey's bag slid down the chute. She moved forward to claim it. Then hurried quickly toward the exit, where a stand of taxis waited.

For once luck was with him. His suitcase was next to bump down the chute. He swung the bag off the conveyor belt and set off after her, self-righteous anger quickening his step. A blast of cold air hit him full in the face, taking his breath away. After the warmth of Florida, returning to the chill of St. Louis was a rude awakening. By the time he caught up with her, she'd already flagged down a taxi; the driver was loading her bags into the trunk.

"Lindsey," he said, grabbing her arm, spinning her around to face him. "I'm tired of all the shots you've been taking at my integrity. I've done nothing to deserve them."

His heart clenched at the tears welling up in her eyes. She stood shivering in the cold, blinking hard, trying not to let the tears flow.

"Talk to me, Lindsey," he said, his tone gentling. "Someone's shaken your trust in men. But it sure in hell wasn't me."

A tear slid down her cheek. Impatiently, she wiped it away. Her voice thick with emotion, she whispered, "Don't pretend you don't know, Alex."

"Know what?"

Her glance flitted over him before finding a safer spot to perch. "You were Danny's best friend."

"Yes, so?" His heart thumped a hollow beat. He felt a prickling of unease, as though he were about to hear something he really didn't want revealed.

"I thought he told you everything." She shook her head, looking embarrassed and miserable. "Danny had an affair, Alex. The man who swore to love only me cheated on me."

Alex felt as though he'd been hit square in the gut. He stared at her, too stunned to speak.

The tears flowed freely now. She did nothing to hide them. Her voice shaking, she said, "You're right, Alex. I am scared. Scared to death that I'll never be able to trust another man's word."

With that, she left him, slipping into the waiting taxi without a backward glance.

This time, Alex did not try to stop her.

She'd barely had time to collect Jamie, stow her suitcase in the bedroom and catch her breath before the front doorbell rang. Lindsey knew who it would be before she opened the door. She wasn't disappointed.

Alex stood on her front porch.

Cold air swirled around her legs. Lindsey shivered, more from trepidation than a November chill. The scowl he wore on his face was enough to send a quiver of fear through any woman's heart.

"You can't just tell me Danny had had an affair while you were married, then walk away," he said, foregoing the usual pleasantries.

Lindsey clung to the doorknob, studying him as a wave of helplessness washed over her. For as long as she'd known Alex, he'd been annoyingly persistent. She'd experienced his single-minded determination first-hand. All those times she'd told him he shouldn't feel obligated to help her and Jamie, but he did anyway. All those time when he'd called just to check on the two of them, and she'd tried to tell him it wasn't necessary. All those times she'd tried to push him away, but he wouldn't budge.

Well, he wasn't budging now.

"Alex, there's nothing you can do," she said quietly, mindful of Jamie nearby. "There's no point in dredging up the past."

"Wrong. Not as long as the past is what's keeping you from trusting me now," he said angrily, the words ringing out loud and clear.

Lindsey shot a furtive glance up and down the quiet tree-lined street, hoping the cold kept her neighbors tucked safely inside their houses. Arguing with a man on her front porch would certainly raise curious eyebrows. She'd endured enough unwanted attention after Danny's death. The last thing she needed was to become the fodder for the neighborhood gossip mill.

Alex continued, oblivious to her growing discomfort. "I didn't know, Lindsey. You have to believe me. Danny never said a word to me about—"

He stopped. Anger flickered across his face. He glanced away and swallowed hard as though he were fighting a personal battle for control.

Lindsey waited, watching him carefully.

When he spoke again, the anger was in check. In its place was an unmistakable bitterness. "When we were younger, Danny had a way of screwing things up, getting himself into more trouble than he could handle. Rick and I always took turns bailing him out. But if he'd come to me, and told me this…I'd never have let him hurt you."

He looked at her then with such sincerity, with such expectancy in his blue eyes, that it made her heart ache. It was reassurance that he sought. The need to know her faith in him was intact.

Goodness only knew, she wanted to believe him.

She wanted to let go of the past.

But she didn't know if that were possible. The pain ran too deep. The memories were too strong. She may never be able to forget…to trust again.

Jamie saved her from having to disappoint him.

"Uncle Alex," he called out, bounding through the living room to greet him. He threw himself into Alex's open arms with an ease that Lindsey envied. He patted the pockets of Alex's leather bomber jacket. "Where's my seashells?"

For the first time that day, a smile lit Alex's handsome face. "Sorry, pardner. I left them in my suitcase. How about if I bring them with me the next time I come?"

Lindsey's breath caught, knowing there might not be a next time.

"Tomorrow? Can you bring them tomorrow?" Jamie persisted.

"We'll see," Alex said, laughing.

A cold breeze whipped across the wraparound porch. Her son's teeth chattered. He shivered and burrowed his face against Alex's neck.

"It's cold out here, isn't it?" Alex said, squeezing him gently. With a sigh, he bent to release him. "You'd better go inside."

"You come inside, too, Uncle Alex." Jamie held on tight. "Play with me."

Wordlessly, Alex looked to her for advice.

That sense of helplessness, as though things were slipping beyond her control, threatened once again. Pushing aside her misgivings, she said, "Of course you're welcome to come in, Alex. Jamie doesn't want you to leave."

Her meaning struck home. She saw that as clearly as

the flinch in Alex's expression. He knew it was for Jamie's sake, not hers, that his stay had been prolonged.

For once she was thankful for her young son's tenacity. As Jamie monopolized Alex's attention for the next thirty minutes, Lindsey busied herself with unpacking, sorting through her mail and pretending not to listen to the pair's conversation. Watching Alex roughhouse with her son, filling a gap in Jamie's fatherless life, yet, knowing his presence may be fleeting, nearly tore her heart in two.

Finally, Jamie lost steam. In the commotion of her unexpected arrival home, he'd missed his afternoon nap. Showing signs of wearing down, he yawned widely in Alex's face.

Alex chuckled. "I think you need to get some sleep, pal."

Jamie didn't bother to argue. Grabbing his favorite blanket, he headed for his bedroom.

"Hey," Lindsey said, shaking her head. "Aren't you going to tell Alex goodbye?"

"G'bye, Uncle Alex," Jamie called over his shoulder. His blanket trailed behind him as he disappeared down the hall.

Lindsey stood awkwardly in the middle of the living room, feeling oddly vulnerable without the safety of her son's presence. "I—I'd better tuck him in."

Alex nodded, his expression grim. He seemed in no hurry to leave.

Sighing, Lindsey left him, following her son to his bedroom. She lingered over her good nights, not anxious to return to the living room, or to Alex. Jamie was fast asleep long before she found the courage to leave him.

Alex was pacing the floor like a caged animal when she rejoined him. He stopped midpace, his gaze flying to hers. The tension sizzled in the room, arcing between them like a lightning bolt of awareness.

Lindsey swallowed hard and chose the safest course of action. She made a beeline for the door. Reaching for the knob, she said, ''It's time for you to leave, Alex.''

His long legs eating up the distance, he quickly caught up with her. He leaned a hand against the door, closing it. ''Not until we've had a chance to talk, Lindsey.''

Slowly she turned to face him. Within inches of touching, her traitorous body reacted. Her pulse quickened. The warm flow of awareness lapped over her. She felt her resistance melting. Refusing to let him see how he'd affected her, she stood her ground. ''There's nothing left to be said, Alex.''

''You're wrong, Lindsey,'' he said, moving closer. ''There's so much more I need to say.''

Not trusting him, not trusting herself, she anchored a staying hand against his chest. Then regretted the action. Through the thin fabric of his polo shirt, she felt the heat of his body and the pulse of his heart, matching hers, unsteady beat for unsteady beat.

She dropped her hand as though it had been burned. ''All right, Alex. If you want me to say I believe you, that you didn't know about Danny's extramarital activities, then fine...I believe you.'' She took in a steadying breath. ''Now, if you don't mind, it's been a long week. I need some time alone.''

''How much time?'' he demanded. ''A week? A year? Or maybe a lifetime.'' His jaw clenched, then unclenched. Impatience flashed in his eyes. She had never seen him react with quite such volatility. ''What Danny did was unforgivable. But you can't judge all men on the basis of one bad experience.''

''I'm not—''

"Yes, you are," he insisted, angling closer still.

Unable to help herself, she stepped back and promptly bumped into the door. His hand still on the door beside her, his large body looming in front of her, he made a formidable roadblock. Trapped, she stared up at him, wide-eyed with uncertainty.

"You can't help the way you feel, Lindsey. You've had a rotten experience with a man you loved," he said. His voice seductively low, it vibrated in her ears, sending shock waves of awareness tripping throughout her body. "But we're not all bad. If you'd give yourself a chance, you just might find that out for yourself."

"Alex—"

He touched a finger to her lips, quieting her. "Don't push me away. Let me show you everything that's been missing from your life." He leaned close, tracing her cheekbone with his fingers. Her skin tingled beneath his touch. "I can be a very good teacher."

Not giving her a chance to protest, he lowered his mouth and claimed her lips. The kiss was gentle, tender, yet thorough. By the time it ended she was breathless and her head was spinning dizzily out of control.

"Lesson number one." He smiled, his white teeth bright against his tanned skin. Cupping a hand around her waist, he brought her snug against the hardness of him. With a devilish glint in his eye, he said, "Lesson number two is twice as nice."

She sucked in a steadying breath. "Alex..."

"Hmm..." he murmured, nuzzling her earlobe and working his way downward.

"Oh, Alex," she sighed, arching her neck to give him better access. What was wrong with her? She had the willpower of a guppy, she chided herself. It was as though she couldn't think rationally whenever he was near. "Alex, I can't..."

His lips skimmed her collarbone. His hands slid beneath her T-shirt, seeking the warmth of her skin.

She shivered and her knees felt like jelly. She collapsed against the door frame. "I can't do this."

His clever fingers sought and found the clasp of her bra. With a practiced move, the closure popped open. She gasped with surprise. Her breasts swelled with anticipation.

Alarm bells sounded in her head. He had undressing a woman down to an art form. Five minutes ago she'd been ready to toss him out on his ear. Now she was melting in his arms. Somehow things had gotten terribly, terribly mixed up.

"Wait," she said, pushing him away as self-control made one final rally. "Just wait a minute."

A pained expression crossed his face. "Now what's wrong?" he demanded, his impatience obvious.

"I have to think about this," she said, trying not to look into those hypnotically blue eyes of his. "I can't just rush into a...a physical relationship."

With a sexy grin, he reached out to reclaim her. "Nobody said anything about rushing. Slow and easy, that's fine with me."

She sidestepped his embrace, putting some much-needed distance between them. "Alex, you're not listening to me."

"I'll be glad to listen, Lindsey," he said. He took a step toward her. "Just tell me what you want."

She opened the door. A shot of air blasted her flushed skin. "I want you to leave."

"Leave?" He stared at the door. Then stared at her, looking confused. "You can't be serious."

"I'm afraid so," she said, shivering more from nervousness than the chill outside. She wrapped her arms around her waist and hugged herself tight. "You're right, Alex. When it comes to men, I'm as inexperienced as they come. But I'm smart enough to realize that I can't just jump into the thick of things with both feet. I need to take baby steps. Tiptoe my way back into this dating game."

"Lindsey, honey," he said, his tone soothing. "You know I'd never hurt you."

"No, not on purpose," she agreed, fighting the sweet lull of his voice. "But the truth is, you don't have all that great of a record with women, Alex. And I don't want to be just another notch on your bedpole."

He frowned. "I told you already—"

"I know, I know…that I can trust you." She took a deep breath. "Well, pardon me for saying so, but I'm just not sure that you deserve my trust. After all, if you really cared about me, why didn't you say anything before? Why keep it such a big secret?"

He opened his mouth to protest.

Only she didn't give him the chance. She continued, the words spilling out before she lost her nerve. "I'll tell you why. It's because you aren't ready for a serious relationship, anymore than I am. If you were, you'd have told me long before now that you wanted more from me than a mere friendship."

He stared at her, the words settling uneasily between them.

Nervously, she licked her lips and forged ahead. "I might be scared of letting a man into my life, Alex. But you're even more petrified of letting a woman into yours. Now if you don't mind…" She shot a pointed glance at the open doorway. "I'd rather not heat the entire neighborhood. My utility bills are high enough as they are."

His eyes narrowed. "This isn't over, Lindsey."

With more confidence than she actually felt, she met his gaze. "I'm not sure it ever started, Alex."

For a long moment neither of them moved. He studied her, his blue eyes penetrating, his expression intimidating. Lindsey resisted the urge to squirm beneath the heavy measure of his gaze.

"Whether you want to believe me or not, you're the woman I want to be with. You always have been," he said finally, with a tone so sincere she couldn't help but want to believe him. "If I have to prove myself to you, then so be it."

Lindsey sighed. "Alex, please—"

He held up both hands in mock surrender. "I'll leave for now, but I promise you, Lindsey. I will be back."

Before she had time to react, he reached out and tugged her into his arms. With a possessiveness that stole her breath, he kissed her. Then, as quickly as it had begun, the kiss ended.

She felt confused and more than a little unbalanced, when—with one last, satisfied grin—he left.

Lindsey slammed the door closed and bolted the lock. Not sure as she did so if she were shutting him out or keeping herself from chasing after him.

Chapter Ten

Two weeks later Lindsey pulled into the parking lot of Kincaid's Antiques. She rubbed her throbbing temples, nursing a king-size headache. Too many sleepless nights had taken their toll; she felt as though she were running on empty.

She blamed Alex for her lack of energy. Alex and his persistent attention. Since returning from Florida, he'd called her daily, visited often, and took her and Jamie out for an occasional dinner. She refused to be alone with him. In general, he was showering her with unwanted attention.

And his pesky tactics were working.

Little by little he was wearing down her defenses. Her reasons not to trust him didn't seem as important whenever he was near. It was only at night, when she was alone and the world was quiet and the past had a chance to sneak back into her mind, that she gave in to the doubts.

Right now, Alex might be showing all the signs of a

man ready to make a commitment, but what made her think he wouldn't change his mind in the future? Deep inside, where her heart was most vulnerable, a part of her was convinced that it was the hunt, not the quarry, that attracted Alex. She represented the unattainable. To him, that made her twice as attractive.

With a sigh, she opened the door of her minivan and stepped outside. After the heat of the car, the cold, frosty air was a shock to her system, nearly taking her breath away. Grabbing the box of tassels from the back seat, she hurried to the store, anxious to get home.

These past two weeks she'd worked overtime to fill Kincaid's order for the Christmas rush. Jamie had been sadly neglected. It was time to get home and spend some quality time with her son.

A bell tinkled overhead as she pushed open the heavy glass-and-wood door. The store felt warm and inviting. It smelled of wood, lemon oil, and leather. Fine oak dressers, massive mahogany chairs and dainty Queen Anne tables filled the shop, all a loving tribute to eras long past.

Moments later, Peter Kincaid stepped out of the back room. Tall and muscular, with a head of thick, curly dark hair, he didn't fit her image of an antique dealer. She couldn't deny the man was attractive. Smiling, he said, "Lindsey, it's good to see you—as always."

She flushed, feeling disconcerted by the intensity of his gaze. In the year since she'd started taking on consignments for Kincaid's Antiques, Peter had made his wishes clear. He wanted more than a working relationship with her. On numerous occasions he'd asked her for a date, all of which she'd declined. His persistence rivaled only Alex's. She was finding it hard to come up with excuses to say no.

Protectively, she held up the box in front of her. "I brought the tassels."

He nodded. "Bring them over, and let me take a look."

Placing the box on the large oak desk that Peter used as his sales counter, Lindsey lifted the lid and began unpacking her work. Carefully wrapped in individual bags and then again in tissue paper, the tassels looked as rich and decadent as a lady's ballgown. Hanging from their satiny strings, they would turn beautiful pieces of furniture into something special.

"Perfect," Peter said, allowing the silky strands to slip through his long fingers. His actions were gentle, loving, as though he were caressing a woman's delicate skin. "These will sell fast."

Lindsey breathed a sigh of relief at his approval. "Great, I could use the money."

His smile deepened. "I think this calls for a celebration. Have dinner with me?"

The automatic refusal rested on the tip of her tongue. But for once, she hesitated. Alex had told her she was inexperienced when it came to men. That much was true. Other than Danny, she hadn't really dated anyone else. Perhaps, it was time she broadened her horizons. Perhaps it was time to prove to Alex she wasn't a novice when it came to the opposite sex.

She forced a smile. "I'd love to."

He looked surprised, almost as shocked as she was by her acceptance. "Tonight?"

"Sorry, I already have a date with my son." She laughed. "I promised Jamie a pizza at Chuck E Cheese's."

"Then tomorrow night," he said firmly, his tone brooking no argument.

Lindsey felt only the slightest bit of unease as she said, "Sure, that'd be fine."

Finishing up the business end of their meeting, she hurried an escape. The cold seeped through her jacket, chilling her to the bone as she strode across the parking lot. Lindsey lifted her collar against the bleakness and slid into the minivan.

Lindsey, Lindsey, Lindsey, what have you done? She knew very well what she'd done. She'd just made a date with a man for whom she had absolutely no feelings, other than a healthy respect for his business acumen.

Grinding the key in the ignition, she popped the car into gear and left Kincaid's Antiques and her second thoughts far, far behind. All the while knowing that it was escaping from Alex and the turbulent emotions he conjured up that had prompted her hasty decision, not any latent attraction to Peter Kincaid.

Alex called late that evening.

It was past ten o'clock. Jamie had fallen asleep hours ago, his tummy filled with pizza and his body exhausted from a night of games and rides.

Lindsey, on the other hand, was wide awake and too keyed up to rest, as she lay in her bed in the dark and waited for Alex to call. She knew it was only a matter of time before she had to face the inevitable. Sooner or later, she would have to tell Alex about her date.

"Sorry I'm calling so late," he said. The din of voices and announcements over an intercom system nearly drowned out his voice. "This is the first chance I've had to get to a phone."

She sat up in bed. The blankets fell away; the cold air nipped at her skin. "Alex, where are you?"

"In Los Angeles," he said. "I'm at the airport."

"Los Angeles?"

"It's a long story. Jon needed some help with our West Coast distributors. So, here I am."

Lindsey shivered, blaming her aging and inefficient heater for her reaction, not the chill of Alex's absence. "When will you be back?"

"I'm not sure," he said. "Maybe tomorrow. More likely Sunday. It all depends on how our meetings go in the morning."

Sunday? Lindsey couldn't believe her good luck. She'd regretted her decision to go out with Peter the minute she'd agreed. If she could come up with a plausible excuse, she'd have canceled right away. The only thing she'd dreaded more than the actual date was Alex finding out.

Now, it would seem, she'd been given a reprieve. She could get this date with Peter over with, and none would be the wiser. None being Alex.

"Lindsey? Are you still there?"

"Yeah, I'm still here."

"Everything all right? You sound a little funny."

"I'm fine," she lied. Guilt flushed her skin. "Just a little tired. I took Jamie to Chuck E Cheese's. My head's still ringing from all the noisy kids."

He chuckled. "This is one time I can honestly say I'm glad I wasn't with you tonight."

"Chicken," she said, unable to stop the grin from forming.

"Hey, I'm crazy about Jamie. It's the thought of dozens of screaming kids I'm not so sure about."

Why did he have to be so understanding when it came to parenting? It only made it that much harder to push him away.

Silence lengthened across the phone line.

Alex was the first to break the stillness.

"Well, I just called...I just called to say hello. And to tell you that I'll be thinking of you."

"Alex—"

"I know, I know, no pressure." He gave a long sigh. "Think of it as just a friendly little reminder. I still care about you, Lindsey. I haven't given up hoping."

An arrow of remorse took direct aim at her heart and struck dead center. Technically, she hadn't lied to Alex, she told herself. Except, perhaps, a lie by omission. Somehow not telling Alex the truth, that she was seeing another man, only made her feel twice as guilty.

His voice softened as he said, "Good night, Lindsey."

"Alex wait!"

"I'm still here."

Lindsey hesitated. What good would it do to tell him? The date meant nothing to her. It was merely an exercise in futility, an obligation that needed to be fulfilled. Alex was alone, halfway across the country. Why make him miserable over nothing?

"Lindsey?"

"I—I just wanted to tell you to be careful."

"I will," he promised. She could almost hear the smile in his voice. "I'll see you soon."

Slowly, Lindsey returned the phone to its receiver. For just a moment she wondered if this was the way Danny had felt when he'd so blithely lied and cheated on her. Like Danny, she'd justified her actions with the adage "what he doesn't know, won't hurt him."

How could she be so cruel?

If Alex found out about her date with Peter, it wouldn't be a matter of whether or not she could trust *him*.

Alex's trust in *her* would be on the line. And she realized she didn't want to take that chance.

"I can handle this," Lindsey muttered to herself as she checked her image in the hall mirror. She'd dressed in black. Not exactly date attire. But appropriate enough for this evening, she assured herself. It matched her mood. Black sweater, black wool skirt, and a string of pearls to offset the gloom.

In ten minutes, or so, Peter Kincaid would be knocking on her door, ready to take her out for the evening. Only, she wouldn't be going. At the last minute she'd canceled the baby-sitter, deciding it best to sit down with Peter and explain why it was she couldn't see him on a social basis. A phone call canceling their date would have been easier, but it seemed so heartless. She wanted to maintain a working relationship with Peter. He had to understand her reasonings.

If only she understood them herself. Lindsey sighed. The truth was, guilt had been a deciding factor. It didn't matter if they'd never had an official date, or whether or not they had a spoken understanding, she couldn't live with herself and be untrue to Alex.

The doorbell rang.

Lindsey froze. Peter was early.

Jamie, dressed in a pair of footed pajamas, lying on the living room's large braided rug, looked up from his set of toy cars. "I get it?"

"No, honey, I'll get it," she said with a confidence she didn't really feel.

She smoothed a hand over the pleats of her skirt and took a deep breath. Pasting a smile on her face, she opened the door. Her smile dissolved as the wrong man greeted her.

Alex stood on her front porch.

He wore a rumpled suit beneath his wool overcoat. His blond hair was unkempt. Dark circles smudged the skin beneath his eyes. The lines of weariness that etched his face were deep and obvious. But a slow smile curved his lips. He looked tired, tousled and irresistibly sexy.

"Alex, what are you doing here?" she demanded.

His smile faded. He raised his brows, taken aback by her greeting. "That's a hell of a way to greet a weary traveler."

"You weren't supposed to be home until tomorrow," she said, unable to keep the accusation from her voice.

"The meeting got out early. I just got back in town. I didn't think you'd mind if I stopped by."

She glanced past his shoulder at the dark and empty street. Then, with an impatient breath, she pulled him inside. "All right, but just for a minute."

He'd already shucked the overcoat and his jacket and was loosening his tie by the time she'd closed the door and turned around. Lindsey squelched a moan. Alex appeared to be a man settling in for the night.

She took in a steadying breath. "Alex, this isn't a good time."

He studied her curiously, his eyes taking in the skirt and sweater, before resting on the pearls. She resisted the urge to squirm beneath his gaze. "Going somewhere?"

"Yes...I mean no," she stammered, feeling the heat rise on her face. She gritted her teeth, annoyed by her skittishness. She was acting like a woman with a guilty secret. But she hadn't done anything wrong...yet. "Alex, why didn't you call first?"

"I didn't realize it would be a problem," he said, with both hands resting on his narrow hips. A defensive expression flickered across his face, as though he were priming himself for battle. She just hoped she wasn't the first casualty.

"Well, it is," she said, shifting uneasily. "I've made other plans."

"Plans?"

Lindsey winced as the single word thundered against the walls of the foyer. She glanced at Jamie, ready to use any means—even her son—to stem the flow of his anger. "Jamie, look who's here. It's Alex."

"Hi, Uncle Alex," Jamie said dutifully. Her uncooperative son glanced up and smiled, then returned his attention to his toy cars, promptly ignoring the foolish adults.

"Lindsey," Alex said, his voice deceptively calm. She could see the fury in his eyes. "You want to tell me what's going on?"

"I—um..." Nervously, she licked her lips. "Well, you see, I have a date."

"The hell you do," he hollered.

Her nervousness vanished in a blaze of self-righteous indignation. How dare he be angry with her over one little, insignificant date? Not when she'd spent the past two years watching him galavant past her with an endless parade of women friends.

"Alex, there's no need to shout," she yelled. "And watch your language. Little ears are listening."

They both glanced at Jamie. Lost in his own world, her son putted like an engine as he ran his car along the makeshift tracks of her braided rug. He hadn't heard a word.

Alex lowered his voice only a fraction. "You're not going!"

"Yes, I am," she countered, ignoring the fact that

she'd already decided to cancel the date in question. "You have no right to tell me what I can and cannot do."

The doorbell rang.

They both froze. The tension in the room was palpable. They glared at each other, daring the other to be the first to move.

Tired of dealing with this impossible example of male pigheadedness, she stamped her foot on the hardwood floor and swirled around to answer the door. She ignored Alex's growl of frustration. Baring her teeth in a semblance of a smile, she threw open the door.

Peter stood on her doorstep, with flowers in his hand and a smile on his lips. The smile faltered when he took one look at her face. "Something wrong?"

"Wrong?" She attempted a lighthearted laugh. It fell flat even to her hopeful ears. "Don't be silly. There's nothing wrong. Come in, Peter."

A scowling Alex still stood in the foyer.

Peter took in Alex's hard, measuring gaze before turning to Lindsey, a silent question in his eyes.

Embarrassed heat blossomed on her face. "Peter Kincaid, this is Alex Trent, an old friend of my late husband's."

Alex's eyes narrowed at her choice of introduction. His manners unfailing, however, he extended a hand to Peter.

The exchange was brief, their expressions assessing. Once over, both men turned perturbed glances to her.

Lindsey wished she could run, not walk, out the front door. Anything to escape this tenuous situation. She sucked in a steadying breath. "Peter, there's been a slight problem. The baby-sitter called and canceled."

Disappointment flickered in Peter's eyes.

A pleased smile touched Alex's lips.

Lindsey set her jaw at a stubborn angle. "But luckily, Alex is available to watch Jamie for me while we're gone." She smiled sweetly. "Isn't that right, Alex?"

She watched the blood rush to Alex's face. He looked furious. "Right," he said, his voice barely in control.

"Then, I'd guess we'd better go. 'Bye, Jamie. Mommy's leaving," Lindsey called, grabbing her coat from the rack before she lost her courage. "We won't be too late, Alex. Jamie'll be ready for bed soon. Enjoy yourself while we're gone."

She opened the door, in a hurry to leave.

Peter, looking confused by the sudden turn of events, didn't follow. Awkwardly, he held out the flowers in his hand.

Sighing, Lindsey snatched them up and handed them to Alex. The poor petals were nearly crushed in his death grip. She looked up into his eyes and shivered at the reflected anger.

Alex was not a happy baby-sitter.

Lindsey had no doubt there'd be hell to pay when she returned from her "date."

Chapter Eleven

Quietly, Alex closed the door to Jamie's room. It hadn't taken long, only an hour after Lindsey left before the boy's eyes had gotten heavy with sleep. He'd talked Jamie into bed with a promise of a nighttime story. Thirty minutes and five books later, Jamie was fast asleep.

Which left Alex with an entire evening to wait for Lindsey's return.

Anger burned slowly in his chest. A soft light shone in Lindsey's bedroom, beckoning him like a beacon. Even as furious as he was with her, he couldn't deny the power she held over him. He wanted her more now than he ever did. He just didn't understand why she felt the need to see someone else.

The bedroom was done in pale peaches and greens. The coverlet was a delicate floral and lace, a reflection of the room's occupant. Alex remembered this being the first thing Lindsey had wanted changed in the house after Danny had died. He and Rick had spent a weekend painting and wallpapering, determined to help in some small way to ease Lindsey's pain.

Only neither of them had realized just how deep, or how lasting that pain might be.

Alex sat down on the bed, picking up a picture that rested on the nightstand. He sucked in a sharp breath, nearly dropping the frame. It was a picture of himself, Danny and Rick. The three musketeers. Inseparable, it would seem, even after death. No matter how much he wanted it to be different, Lindsey would always see him in the same light as Danny.

They'd been friends, confidants. They'd shared similar likes and dislikes. Hell, they'd even shared the same taste in women. Lindsey was certainly proof of that.

It wasn't any wonder she'd be reluctant to settle down with a man who reminded her so much of a husband that had cheated on her.

Alex's grip tightened on the picture, his knuckles turning white from the exertion. *Dammit, Danny. Why couldn't the problems you'd caused in your life die right along with you?*

He felt an instant guilt at the thought. Stunned by his own fury, Alex dropped the picture back onto the nightstand. He stood, thrusting his balled hands into his pants' pockets, uncertain what to do next.

The room smelled of lavender and springtime, Lindsey's scent. A silky bathrobe lay at the end of the bed, ready to be slipped on for the night. Her hairbrush stood on the dresser. He imagined her using it, with soft, gentle strokes. Everywhere he looked, he was bombarded with images of Lindsey. She was so close, just a whisper away from touching.

Yet she'd never felt so damn far away.

Alex snapped off the bed lamp, casting the room into darkness. It seemed almost as bleak as his heart.

The phone rang.

Glad for the interruption, Alex strode from the room, heading for the kitchen to answer the call. His relief was short-lived. Lindsey's brother, Rick, was on the phone.

"Where's Lindsey?" Rick asked with his usual bluntness.

"Out," Alex answered curtly, knowing the man on the other line could read him better than anyone. It was best to keep the conversation short, rather than let his friend guess the reason for his foul mood. "I'm baby-sitting Jamie."

"I see," Rick said slowly. "My sister's out on a Saturday night, and you're stuck at home playing nursemaid to my nephew. Let me guess—Lindsey's on a date."

Alex swore softly beneath his breath.

"The antique dealer, right?"

Ignoring the question, Alex said, "I'll have Lindsey call when she gets back."

Rick chuckled. "Do you know when she'll be back?"

"No, I do not," he said, keeping a firm grip on his temper. "Now, if there's nothing else—"

"How long are you going to let this go on, Alex?"

Alex kneaded the tender spot between his brows, hoping to relieve the pounding in his aching head. "I don't know what you're talking about, Rick."

"I'm talking about Lindsey. You've been carrying around one hell of a torch for my baby sister. When are you going to break down and tell her how you feel?"

Alex leaned a hip against the kitchen counter and sighed. "I already did. She wasn't interested."

A thoughtful silence stretched across the phone line.

"I know my sister. She's interested. There's something you aren't telling me, isn't there?"

Alex didn't say a word.

"Is it Danny?"

"No," he said quickly. Too quickly. Alex winced at the desperate sound of his own voice.

Rick continued. "Because if it is, she's wasting her time. Danny's gone. Grieving isn't going to bring him back."

"I wish it were that simple," Alex murmured.

"You're not giving up, are you?"

Alex sighed again, uncertain how to answer.

"Because there's no way I want to see my sister end up with a furniture salesman. You've got to do something to change her mind, and do it fast."

Alex rolled his eyes. "Look, Rick, I'm doing my best. Lindsey's the one who isn't cooperating."

"Damn, what else can go wrong with this family?" Rick released a slow, whistling breath. "I thought my sister had better sense than I did."

Alex frowned. He'd never heard his friend sound so down, so defeated. "What are you talking about, Rick? What's going on?"

Rick hesitated, then, in a flat, emotionless voice said, "The letter I wrote—the one about the police department's policy of looking the other way when a relative of a city official breaks the law—the local newspaper's doing a feature article on it. It'll be in the Sunday paper. They thought it might stir up a little political controversy."

"You're kidding?"

"Wish I were." He gave a dry, mirthless laugh. "I thought the whole thing was going to blow over with me getting just a slap on the wrist. But the department's

already gotten wind of the story. I've been called in for
a disciplinary meeting first thing Monday morning.''

"Jeez, Rick. Is there anything I can do?"

"Tell Lindsey. I don't want her to be shocked when
she reads the morning paper.''

"Sure, anything you want.' Alex said the words feeling hopelessly inadequate. "Rick, the offer of my family's cabin in the mountains is still open. Colorado's a
great place to unwind this time of year. No newspapers.
No TV. Nothing to do but watch the snow fly.''

Rick dragged in a ragged breath. "Thanks, Alex. I'll
keep it in mind. In the meantime, talk some sense into
that sister of mine. She's long overdue for a little happiness in her life. I'm depending on you to see that she
gets it.''

"Yes, sir.'' Alex chuckled. "I'll do my best.''

In a voice that carried more than a bit of a threat, Rick
added, "Oh, and your best had better include making an
honest woman of her. Or you'll be answering to me.''

"Right," Alex said.

He hung up the phone, feeling oddly reassured. He'd
been a part of Lindsey's life since she was in junior high.
He knew her better than anyone, including Rick.
Whether she wanted to admit it or not, there was no man
better qualified for the job of making Lindsey happy than
himself.

He fully intended to keep that job for a very long time,
say for a lifetime.

Alex scowled. He was in love with the fool woman.
Just as soon as she got back from her *date,* he'd tell her
so himself.

Lindsey toyed with the pasta on her plate, unable to
swallow a bite. No matter how hard she tried, she

couldn't forget the look on Alex's face when she'd left. That hurt, abandoned look. She took in a shaky breath. She didn't blame him for being upset. Making him baby-sit while she went out on a date with another man was a very, very cruel thing to do.

"I found it while vacationing in the south of France," Peter said. "It was a very fine piece, a Louis the Four-teenth."

Lindsey nodded, half listening to the conversation as she jabbed her fork at an artichoke. The date was an unmitigated disaster. Peter was a nice enough man. He was polite, well-spoken and intelligent. But he just wasn't...Alex.

"Of course, I had a terrible time getting it away from the space aliens."

Lindsey smiled politely. She wondered what Alex was doing right now. The thought of him wandering around her big, empty house all alone sent a quiver of appre-hension through her heart. Not that she didn't trust him. He wasn't the type to steal the silver, if she had any silver. No, it just conjured up such a lonely picture.

"Those green little men just wouldn't sell."

Absently, she ran a finger over the rim of her water glass. She'd gotten herself into sticky situations before, but this one really topped them—

"Lindsey," Peter said, a touch of impatience in his tone.

She blinked, glancing up at him with startled eyes.

"Have you heard a word I've said?"

Her face warmed with embarrassment. "Of course, a Louis the Fourteenth, right?"

"Right." He shook his head and smiled. "As much as I wish it were with me, your mind's miles away... with another man, perhaps?"

"Of course not..." She started to protest.

"Lindsey, I'd have to blind not to notice there was something going on between you and this old friend of yours. Alex, wasn't it?"

She placed her fork on her plate and sighed. "I'm sorry, Peter."

"Don't be. I'm the one who's sorry." He raised an eyebrow, a question in his eyes. "Is it serious between you and this...Alex?"

Lindsey frowned, searching for the right words. "Things are a little complicated at the moment. Alex and I are dealing with a few unresolved issues."

"And my being with you tonight has complicated these issues even more?"

Lindsey grimaced. "Slightly."

Peter placed his napkin on the table and motioned to the waiter. "I think it's time I took you home."

"No, really, Peter—"

"Yes, really, Lindsey," he said, his voice determined. "I'm too selfish to share my evening with a beautiful woman. Especially when I'm competing against a man who isn't even here."

"I'm sorry," Lindsey mumbled, wondering how the evening could get any worse. An image of Alex's stormy face popped into her mind, and then she knew.

Alex would still be waiting for her when she returned home.

"Check, please," Peter told the waiter as he joined them. He chuckled, turning his attention to Lindsey. "Believe me, Lindsey. You have nothing to be sorry about. It's amazing what a stroke to the ego it is to know you are the cause of another man's jealousy."

"You're very sweet," she said. "Your understanding is the last thing I deserve."

He covered her hand with his. "You deserve to be happy, Lindsey. If this Alex is the one to make you happy, then so be it. But if he isn't, then I'll be back to finish this date."

The question of her happiness with Alex might just be a moot point, Lindsey mused. After what she'd done to him tonight, it would be a miracle if he was still talking to her.

Her chest tightened at the thought. It hurt when she drew in a breath. Feeling close to tears, she swore softly.

As usual, she was the last to see the truth, even though it had been standing right in front of her nose. She'd fallen in love with Alex. It wasn't any wonder that she'd been running scared.

Peter held open the door of his Mercedes.

Giving him a polite smile, Lindsey stepped outside. The sky was spitting snow. Her breath came in thick, foggy plumes, crystallizing almost as soon as it escaped into the air. The cold nipped her nose and stung her cheeks, making her long for the warmth of the Florida sunshine. She'd been happy there...before Alex turned her world upside down.

Their footsteps echoed against the brick sidewalk, sounding even louder on the wooden front porch. If Alex didn't know that they were home yet, he surely knew now. Lindsey fumbled in her purse for her key.

She needn't have bothered.

The door flew open. Warmth and light poured out through the doorway. Alex stood waiting for her.

Lindsey stared at him, agitation mixing with apprehension. The last man who'd dared to meet her at the door at the end of a date had been her father. The cool, challenging glare her father had served on all of her beaus hadn't been any less intimidating than Alex's was now.

Peter touched her arm, the gesture protective. "You want me to come inside?" he murmured.

She shook her head, knowing she had nothing to fear from what awaited her inside. It was the fear in her own heart that worried her most. "I'll be fine."

Peter narrowed a measuring glance at Alex.

Alex met the challenge head-on.

Men. Lindsey rolled her eyes, taking the matter into her own hands. "Good night, Peter."

Reluctantly he agreed. "Good night, Lindsey."

Lindsey stood on the porch, with the wind and the snow whipping around her, watching as Peter hurried down the steps to his car. Prickles of awareness skittered down her spine as she felt the heavy weight of Alex's gaze.

Slowly, she turned to face him. Their eyes locked and held. Neither of them moved until Peter's car roared to life. Alex glanced at the street, watching as the Mercedes pulled away. His expression grim, he stepped back, allowing her entry.

As he shut the door, she dared a closer glance. The tie was long gone. His shirtsleeves were rolled up, exposing the sinewy muscles of his forearms. If possible, he looked even more tired than before. But he still looked dangerously irresistible.

"How's Jamie?" she asked, searching for an end to the echoing silence.

"Asleep," Alex said, his answer short, his tone curt.

He wasn't going to make this easy for her, Lindsey realized. Not that she deserved anything less. What she had done was beyond forgiveness. She'd allowed her fears to get the better of her. She'd run away from the one man who had never disappointed her.

Despite the warmth of the house, she shivered. She wrapped her arms around her waist and hugged them tightly, burrowing herself into the safety of her coat.

"How was your *date?*"

"My date was—" Her breath caught as he stepped toward her. "Short."

"That's too bad," he said with a total lack of sincerity. He reached out and slipped the coat from her shoulders, letting it fall to the floor with a thud. He stood so close she could see the dark whiskers of his late-day beard; she could smell the spicy scent of his aftershave and hear the ragged inhalations of his breath.

"Meeting me at the door wasn't necessary," she said as the room tilted. She felt dizzy, out of control. Swaying slightly, she reached for something to balance her. Unfortunately, Alex was the only thing nearby. Lightning bolts of awareness shot up her hand as her fingers grazed his arm.

"Think nothing of it." He brought a steadying hand to her waist. And she wished he hadn't. Her knees began to wobble. "Too bad Petie boy had to leave so fast. He forgot to collect his good-night kiss."

Breathlessly, Lindsey said, "Maybe he just didn't want an audience."

"Maybe he just wanted to leave in one piece," he whispered. He cupped his free hand to the back of her neck. Weaving his fingers through her thick, dark curls, he tipped her head back to face him. The gesture was possessive and brash, a man about to stake his claim.

She felt a trembling of anticipation, wondering if she were merely seeing a reflection of her own desire in his shimmering eyes.

He took her lips then, with a kiss that warmed the chill from her heart. Parting her lips with a single stroke of his tongue, he delved into her mouth, tasting, seeking, possessing.

And Lindsey came alive in his arms.

Heat and desire collided. With a moan of surrender, she pressed her curves against his hard body, feeling the need to be close. She thought she'd lost him and his friendship. Second thoughts were a dim and quickly fading memory. All that mattered was having his arms around her and the feel of him holding her tight.

Much too soon, he pulled away. Swearing softly, he tore his mouth from hers. "Lindsey, I—"

She felt his withdrawal like the rush of a cold, frosty breeze. Growling her impatience, she raked her fingers through his blond hair and pulled him down for another kiss.

He complied without complaint.

Their mouths melded, mating in a rhythm as old as time. Each giving and taking pleasure equally. The roar of passion and their labored breaths were the only sounds to be heard in the empty room. Until, gasping for air, they broke apart.

"I've changed my mind," Lindsey said, puffing an errant hair from her eyes. "You're allowed to meet me at the door any time I have a date."

"There won't be any more dates," he said sternly. He narrowed a gaze. "Tell me you won't be seeing the antique dealer, again."

"Alex, Alex, Alex, what am I going to do with you?" she asked, striving for a lighthearted tone. She wasn't sure if she was ready to take on anything more serious than the glint in his eye. "These caveman tactics have got to stop—"

"Lindsey."

The single word, while said lightly, carried the weight of the world. It was the expression on his face, the quiet determination that told her she was fighting a losing battle. Lindsey sighed. She loved him. He had every right to ask for her loyalty.

"I won't be seeing Peter again…except on a business basis." Frowning, she added, "That is, if he's still willing to sell my work. After tonight, I wouldn't be surprised if he dropped me from his sales books like yesterday's dirty laundry."

"Good."

She frowned. "You know, Alex. You're really starting to annoy me. This is my life's work we're talking about. I still have a living to make. Bills to pay. A child to feed."

"That won't be a problem," he said calmly. "I plan to help from now on."

She stepped out of his embrace. "Oh, no, you won't. I've told you before I don't need your help. I don't need anyone's help. I can take care of Jamie on my—"

"Lindsey, I want to marry you."

Not a question.

Not, *Lindsey, will you marry me?*

But a quiet, determined statement.

She pressed a hand to her fluttering stomach. "W-what did you say?"

He smiled, an irritatingly smug smile. "I said, I want to marry you."

The room began to spin. She got the impression of time slipping by at a lightning speed. As though things were happening much too fast.

"You…" Then, surprising both of them, she whacked

the flat of her palm against the solid wall of his chest. "You jerk!"

He blinked. "What'd you do that for? All I said was—"

"I know, I know, you want to marry me," she hollered.

"You're angry?" His eyes widened in disbelief. "I don't believe it. I thought you'd be pleased. You were the one who said I couldn't make a commitment." He ran a hand through his hair, looking frustrated and more than a bit peeved. "Well, asking a woman to marry me is a pretty damn big commitment. At least, in my book anyway."

She glared at him. "Exactly when did you make this decision, Alex? Tonight?"

He shifted uncomfortably, one foot to the other. "Well, no…"

"Ha! If it wasn't for my date with Peter, you'd never have gotten around to mentioning it." She threw up her hands in disgust, feeling her emotions bubbling out of control. "I know you, Alex. You would have hemmed and hawed around the issue for the next few months, waiting for the right moment to tell me. Only there never would be a right moment. And nothing would have changed." Unexpected tears welled up in her eyes, blurring her vision. "You'll never change."

"Lindsey," he said, looking stricken. He moved closer, reaching for her. "I never meant to upset you. You know I hate it when you cry."

"Yeah, well, you'd better leave now, while the going's good." She sniffed loudly, moving away from him, heading for the safety of the living room. "Because I feel a whole bucket of tears coming on."

"Uh-uh," he said, shaking his head, setting his jaw

in a stubborn line. He continued his frontal assault, closing the gap between them. "Not this time. I'm not leaving here until we get this settled." He pointed a finger at his chest. "I'm not the only one to blame, this time. You're the one who went out with this...this antique dealer."

She lifted her trembling chin. "I had a perfectly reasonable explanation for going out with Peter."

"This I have to hear," he growled.

The backs of her legs bumped against the sofa. Lindsey stumbled to a stop, guilt and discomfort spreading like a heat rash. Her skin itched beneath the folds of her heavy wool sweater. "Well, Peter asked. And I...I—"

"Said yes," he finished for her, emotion glinting in his eyes. "All the while knowing how much I cared about you. Pardon me for saying so, Lindsey, but I'm not the only one in this room with a problem of avoidance."

"All right," she said, frustration churning inside her chest. "Going out with Peter was a stupid thing to do. And maybe, just maybe, I'm afraid to admit my feelings. But can you blame me? Every time I trust a man, they seem to find a way to disappoint me."

"So you weren't going to give me the chance to disappoint you," he said, his voice unnervingly calm. "You were going to push me away before I could get any closer."

"Yes...I mean no." Confusion muddied her mind. She sank down onto the couch, feeling tired and defeated. Good grief, she'd made such a mess of things. "I don't know what I was trying to do."

The couch listed beneath his weight as he sat beside her. "You were scared, Lindsey. You were afraid of being hurt." He sighed. "I don't blame you. After what you've been through, you have a right to be cautious."

She shot him a wan smile. "Would it help any if I told you I had planned to cancel my date with Peter?"

He frowned. "Cancel? But—"

"I'd already told the baby-sitter not to come," she admitted. "I was going to tell Peter I couldn't go, then you knocked on the door and—"

"And I, fool that I am, went into a jealous rage and forced your hand." He shook his head, giving a mirthless laugh. "What's wrong with us, Lindsey? At this rate, we'll never get together."

"Are you sure that's what you want?" Nervously, she licked her lips, her mouth suddenly feeling dry. "Our being together?"

"I've never wanted anything more in my life," he said, his tone adamant. "I love you, Lindsey. I'm not afraid to admit I've loved you for a very long time. I can't imagine a world without you in it."

Weeks of confusion vanished in a steamy flush of relief. "I love you, too," she said, her voice a hoarse whisper. "I think I've always loved you. You've always been my friend, Alex. You've never let me down. No one has ever made me feel more secure, or more alive."

His blue eyes searched her face. "Do you trust me?"

She nodded, not trusting herself to speak. She swallowed hard at the lump of emotion in her throat. "With all my heart."

"Thank God for that." The tension seemed to seep from his body. His muscles relaxed. His face softened. He took her hand, pressing it against his lips. "Lindsey, I've waited a long time to ask you this. I'll be damned if I'm going to let it go a minute longer. Will you marry me?"

She hesitated only for a moment. "Yes, Alex. I'll marry you."

He closed his eyes and gave a sigh of relief. "Finally."

Then, with a whoop of joy, he hauled her into his arms.

"Alex," she scolded, her heart thumping. She pressed a finger to his lips. "You'll wake Jamie."

"I don't care," he said, a goofy grin spreading across his face. "I don't care if I wake up the whole damned neighborhood. You're going to be my wife. Nothing else matters."

Showering her lips, her face, her neck with butterfly kisses, slowly he lowered her down onto the couch. He settled himself next to her, pulling her snug against him.

She shivered with delight, the world seeming perfect and right.

His breath tickling her skin, he asked, "How about next week?"

"Hmm?" she murmured, gasping as his fingertips traced the outline of her breast, working its way downward to the curve of her hip.

"For the wedding," he said, nibbling on her earlobe, slipping a hand beneath her sweater.

She sat up abruptly, nearly knocking him off the couch. "Alex, we can't get married next week."

"Why not?" he asked, looking peeved.

"Because your family's in Florida. Mine's in St. Louis. With logistics like that, we'd never get a wedding ready on that short notice. Besides, your sister's still hurting from her broken engagement. It'd be cruel to plan our wedding so soon after her own wedding disaster."

Alex sighed, and Lindsey knew he understood. "If not next week, then when?"

Lindsey bit her lip, considering. "Valentine's Day has always been one of my favorite holidays."

"Lindsey—" He didn't look happy.

"And this may sound crazy, but I'd like to get married in Florida, a sunset service on the beach."

"Florida?"

She smiled, a half-sheepish little grin. "Remember after Stephanie's wedding rehearsal? The church parking lot?"

He nodded.

"The sunset was so beautiful, glittering off the water, and…" She sighed. "And that's when I knew my life would never be the same. That my feelings for you had changed."

He smiled, his eyes darkening with emotion. "Florida it is."

"It wouldn't have to be large—just our families, and maybe Sandy next door and her brood—"

"Lindsey, invite whomever you want. Hell, I'll fly the whole damn city of St. Louis to Florida, just as long as you marry me."

"On Valentine's Day?"

She watched the thunderclouds gather across his face. "Valentine's Day is almost two months away."

"It'd give Stephanie some time to recover…time for us to make our plans…"

He raised a questioning brow. "Time for you to change your mind?"

"Never." She reached for him, tugging him into her arms. "You've asked me to marry you. You've promised to spend the rest of your life loving only me." She brushed her lips against his, and felt the soft inhalation of his breath. "I plan to hold you to that promise."

He kissed her then. A sweet and tender kiss.

She surrendered herself to his gentle embrace, knowing that she had nothing to fear from this man who swore to be faithful. The mistakes of the past would not be repeated. Trusting Alex would be as easy and as natural as breathing, as living.

She had a lifetime to prove this to be true.

Epilogue

A brisk wind swept the beach, whipping the minister's robe, nearly drowning out his baritone voice. "We are gathered here today to join this man and this woman in holy wedlock…"

Alex had waited a lifetime to hear those words. Now that the moment had arrived, he could hardly believe it was true. His heart hammered in his chest, competing with the pounding of the surf. Cautiously, he hazarded a glance at his bride.

Lindsey stood next to him, a contented smile on her strawberry-colored lips. The wind brushed a strand of her dark hair across her face. Casually, she raked the errant curl aside. She wore a simple white dress with a flowing skirt that swirled about her slender legs. Her feet were bare and unfettered, her toes buried in the sand. Unlike himself, she looked calm and at peace.

Alex felt an unexpected flicker of exasperation. It didn't seem quite fair that, with all the trouble it took for him to finally get her to agree to this wedding, he should be the one suffering from a case of pre-wedding jitters.

Between them, Jamie squirmed, fidgeting with the bow of his tie, drawing Alex's attention from his bride.

Alex placed a calming hand on the boy's shoulder. Jamie looked up, squinting a glance at him. Alex winked and gave him a quick smile. The contact had a soothing effect. Jamie stopped fidgeting and concentrated on the ministers' words.

Just in time, too. The minister's voice boomed, demanding his attention. "Do you, Alex Hale Trent, take this woman to be your lawfully wedded wife..."

Emotion caught in his throat as he listened to the words. Breathing deeply, Alex found the strength to answer, "I do."

In a clear and concise voice, Lindsey repeated the vow.

With a satisfied nod, the minster turned to the best man. "The rings, please."

Jon didn't move.

Alex frowned, glancing at his brother. Jon's attention was focused on his wife, Rachel. In the three months since Thanksgiving, his brother and his wife had settled their differences. So much so, they were behaving like a pair of lovesick teenagers. None too gently, Alex nudged his brother.

"The rings, please," the minister repeated, louder this time.

Fumbling, Jon fished the pair of rings out of his jacket's breast pocket and handed them to Alex. In turn, Alex handed the rings to the minister.

The minister gave Jon a quizzical glance before turning his attention to the bride. "Lindsey, repeat after me.

Alex, take this ring as a sign of my everlasting love and fidelity…''

The vow hit home with a powerful force. Alex had been witness to so many other weddings in which he'd taken the pledge of faithfulness for granted. Since falling in love with Lindsey, he had learned the importance of those words. For the first time that evening, Lindsey's hands shook as she placed the ring on his finger.

''Alex, repeat after me. Lindsey, take this ring…''

In a voice that was somber and sincere, Alex repeated the vow. Feeling the tremor in her hand as he held it in his, he hesitated for a moment before slipping the ring on her finger.

With an uncertain look in her eyes, Lindsey met his gaze. And in that moment he knew she understood just how much he loved her. The fear in her eyes disappeared. A smile lit her beautiful face.

Alex slipped the gold ring on her finger.

''By the power vested in me, I pronounce you husband and wife,'' the minister declared. With a smile, he turned to Alex and said, ''You may kiss the bride.''

A cheer of approval arose from the small crowd gathered on the beach as Alex swept Lindsey into his arms and complied with the minister's directions.

Amidst the rounds of congratulations from their families, another gust of wind buffeted the beach, setting their guests shivering. Alex's father announced, ''Time to go inside.'' He nodded in the direction of the sun that had turned the sky into a vivid palate of pinks and purples. ''Once that sun goes down, the temperature's going to sink like a rock. An outdoor wedding on Valentine's Day is a little too temperamental even by Florida standards.''

Taking Lindsey's arm, Alex escorted his wife inside.

His sister, Stephanie, and Lindsey's brother, Rick, strode past them, their arms linked, both deep in conversation...with Stephanie doing most of the talking, however.

"Now, if I were you," Stephanie said. "I wouldn't hesitate to appeal the police board's disciplinary action. They had no right to punish you for writing that letter to the editor. Six months of desk duty! If that isn't the silliest thing I've ever heard. Your right to free speech is at jeopardy. Trust me, you've got a strong case, Rick. Now, when I get settled in St. Louis—"

Alex grinned as Rick grimaced, giving him a helpless glance. It had been decided that Stephanie would be joining her brothers at Lobo Shoes as their corporate attorney. The company could use a shot of his sister's vivacious energy. As Alex knew she would, Stephanie had survived the break up of her engagement to Jeffrey. Her former fiancé was now a distant and unpleasant memory.

Rick turned his attention to Stephanie, gazing into her sparkling eyes. His hand lingered at her waist, as her heeled foot stumbled. Alex shook his head. In more ways than one, Rick was a captive audience.

As the newlyweds stepped into the living room, where their families were gathered, they were handed glasses of champagne by a white-jacketed waiter.

A hush fell on the crowd as Jon lifted his glass in tribute to the newlyweds.

"When Alex told me he was getting married, my first reaction was...it's about time."

A tittering of laughter accompanied his remark. Everyone but Alex was smiling. Lindsey gave his arm a reassuring squeeze.

"When he told me he was marrying Lindsey, I

said…thank God." Jon turned to his new sister-in-law. "I can't think of a better woman for the job. If anyone can keep my brother in line, it's you, Lindsey."

Lindsey blushed becomingly.

Alex sent his brother a smoldering glance.

Jon placed a hand on the head of the tow-headed hellion, Jamie. "When you joined our family, Lindsey, we acquired a package deal. A new sister and a nephew. Jamie, my man, you told me a secret this morning that you said I could share with everyone today. He said he's asking Santa Claus for a little brother for Christmas. Lindsey, Alex, that means you've exactly nine months to see to his wish. Happy honeymoon, brother."

Laughter erupted from the group.

Lindsey's eyes widened.

Alex ran a finger beneath his collar, clearing his throat as the heat of embarrassment rose on his face.

Then Jon focused his attention on his wife. "But don't worry, Alex. If you don't quite meet the deadline, then Jamie's going to have to settle for a cousin to play with instead. Even if, he or she, is only a couple of months old. Right, Rachel?"

Rachel nodded, flushing with pleasure as whoops of surprise sounded in the room. After accepting a round of congratulations, Jon tipped his champagne glass to the newlyweds. "Seriously, I wish both of you a lifetime of happiness, a love that will never die and a marriage that will be long and fruitful. I can't think of two people who deserve it more."

A murmur of agreement echoed from the crowd. Glasses were raised and drained. Alex's grip tightened at Lindsey's waist. He looked at her and saw the tears in her eyes.

He leaned close, whispering in her ear, catching the

delicate scent of her perfume. "Tell me those are tears of happiness."

"What else?" She smiled, blinking rapidly to stave the flow.

"I love you, Lindsey. I always will. You'll never have a reason to doubt me, I promise."

"I know," she said with a contented sigh. She brushed a finger along the side of his jaw, sending a trembling of emotion rising deep inside him. "Kiss me, Alex. I'm feeling sadly neglected."

"A neglected bride on her wedding day?" Alex grinned. "We certainly can't have that."

Ignoring the catcalls from the crowd, Alex swept his wife into his arms and kissed her soundly.

* * * * *

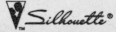

#1 *New York Times* bestselling author

NORA ROBERTS

Presents a brand-new book in the beloved MacGregor series:

THE WINNING HAND
(SSE#1202)

October 1998 in

Silhouette®SPECIAL EDITION®

Innocent Darcy Wallace needs Mac Blade's protection in the high-stakes world she's entered. But who will protect Mac from the irresistible allure of this vulnerable beauty?

**Coming in March, the much-anticipated novel,
THE MacGREGOR GROOMS
Also, watch for the MacGregor stories
where it all began!**

**December 1998:
THE MacGREGORS: Serena—Caine**

**February 1999:
THE MacGREGORS: Alan—Grant**

**April 1999:
THE MacGREGORS: Daniel—Ian**

Available at your favorite retail outlet, only from

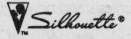

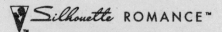

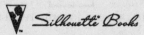

COMING NEXT MONTH

#1324 THE NINE-MONTH BRIDE—Judy Christenberry
Virgin Brides

It was supposed to be a marriage with just one objective—to make a baby! Or so Lucas Boyd and Susannah Langston thought. But the more time Susannah spent in Lucas's arms, the more he hoped to convince her that the real purpose was…love.

#1325 WEDDING DAY BABY—Moyra Tarling

They'd shared one passionate night eight months ago. But now naval officer Dylan O'Connor had no memory of that night—and Maggie Fairchild had an all-too-apparent reminder. Could Maggie rekindle their love before the stork arrived?

**#1326 LOVE, HONOR AND A PREGNANT BRIDE
—Karen Rose Smith**
Do You Take This Stranger?

Penniless and pregnant, young Mariah Roswell had come to rancher Jud Whitmore with the news of his impending fatherhood. But would the man who'd lovingly taken her virginity take her into his heart and make her his true-love bride?

#1327 COWBOY DAD—Robin Nicholas
Men!

Pregnant single mom Hannah Reese had learned the hard way that not all cowboys lived up to a code. Then she met rodeo star Devin Bartlett. Rough, rugged, reliable, he made her feel…and dream…again. Could *he* be the perfect cowboy dad—and husband?

#1328 ONE PLUS ONE MAKES MARRIAGE—Marie Ferrarella
Like Mother/Like Daughter

Gruff Lancelot Reed never thought he'd love again—until Melanie McCloud came crashing into his life. Lance wanted to have nothing in common with this spirited woman, but the intense attraction he felt for her was more than even he could deny….

**#1329 THE MILLIONAIRE MEETS HIS MATCH
—Patricia Seeley**
Women To Watch

Millionaire Gabe Preston didn't know what to think of beautiful Cass Appleton when she landed on his property, searching for her missing cat. But as the fur flew between them, Gabe started hoping he could help her find something else—love.